THE ROGUE CODE

TERRY MARCHION

The Rogue Code Copyright © 2020 by Terry Marchion. All Rights Reserved.

Cover design by Danielle Annett - Coffee & Characters

Visit my website at:
www.TerryMarchion.com

❦ Created with Vellum

For my family, without whom my imagination would stagnate.

Visit my webpage: www.terrymarchion.com .
While there, sign up to receive free sneak peeks, advance notice of upcoming releases and much more fun things to come.

Visit me on Facebook: www.facebook.com/TerryMarchionAuthor

Instagram:
www.instagram.com/TerryM66

1

Tremain reached forward and twisted a dial on the dashboard before him. A rush of cool air filled the cabin of his rented autonomous car.

He was returning from a vacation. That phrase and his name were usually not combined, and he chuckled to himself at the silliness of it all.

It's not that his vacation wasn't deserved, or welcome. After the events of the past few years, he needed some time off. Time to re-adjust and re-assess his life.

So, he'd gone to the beach.

The beach south of the city.

The beach near the gulf which always received plenty of hot sun and tropical breezes.

The beach just everyone wanted to visit. It would be crowded, yes, but the time off would do him good.

Well, it would have been better had the locals not insisted on pronouncing 'New Earth' as 'N'earth', slurring the two words like they had never been separate in the first place. He gritted his teeth every time he heard it uttered. In the interest of his vacation, however, he did his best to ignore that offense to his ears and the spoken language, and tried to enjoy himself.

He relaxed as he sat in the sun, sipping cold beverages, letting the cares of the world drift away. At one point, he fancied that he could actually feel his worries burn away…

No, that was sunburn.

Ouch.

A day of staying out of said sun and lathering up in burn cream seemed to help, but soon it was time to leave. The Colony Days celebration was to start in the next few days and Tremain had a seat for a symposium on a subject he was greatly interested in; Society and how it changes with Technology, or something like that, he couldn't quite remember.

He also had a television interview set up. He couldn't quite remember when that was, but Solomon, the resident AI, should have that saved somewhere. Near photographic memory only works when one actually *wants* to remember something.

He stretched in the roomy cab of the driver-less car, hearing the soft creak of the leather seat as he shifted, soft music playing over the whine of the electric engine. The cab, bathed in a blue-green glow from the heads-up display being projected onto the windshield, now sat at a comfortable 72 degrees. The display, impressive in these newer models, showed rate of speed, outside weather, a small GPS map of the route back to Capitol City, with options for news headlines, music selections, etc., all without impeding the view out the windshield.

Plus, he thought, it still had that new-car smell about it.

All-in-all, a luxurious ride.

The monotony of sitting and riding, coupled with the hypnotizing motion of the white lines in the roadway, lulled Tremain into drowsiness.

In his slumber, he dreamed he was back in the valley of the Mayflower people, watching the water as it spewed through the opening in the mountain, the same river which had carved out the entire valley thousands of years ago. He sat in peace, the only person around, except for a bird that seemed to be perched right near his ear, chirping.

Chirp.

Chirp.

Beep.

Beep.

Beep.

BEEP.

Waking up, he realized the incessant noise didn't come from a bird, but an alarm from the navigation system. Sitting up straighter, and reluctantly opening his eyes, he glared at the dash. The entire on-screen display flashed red, not a good sign at all, with one message blinking in his direct line of sight: Signal lost, please engage manual mode.

Signal lost?

Signal...

Lost...?

Was that even possible?

How does one even engage manual mode?

Manual mode!

The car slowed as the auto systems disengaged. Tremain noticed a flashing dotted line leading from the message on screen, down the center of the dashboard, around the entertainment controls, to a flashing button upon which the words 'manual override' were prominently printed. Offering up a silent prayer to whatever Gods existed, or whichever ones cared to listen for that matter, he pressed it.

Two pedals raised from the floor in front of him as the dash opened to reveal an emerging steering wheel and column. Tremain grasped the wheel and stamped on the accelerator. The car shot forward.

A million questions ran through his mind, ranging from how did humanity ever exist without driver-less vehicles, to how in the world could all the satellites lose signal at once?

He over-corrected as he swerved to miss another car that had turned into his lane, the driver frantic in his attempts to control his own vehicle. Looking beyond his immediate surroundings, he noticed other cars doing the same thing; swerving to miss collisions.

So, it wasn't just his car that had lost signal.

He didn't have much time to dwell on it as he swerved to avoid a container truck full of chickens (as indicated by the verbiage on the side, and the frightened clucking coming from within, not to mention the flurry of feathers pouring from the rear). Tremain over-corrected again, spinning into the median between opposing lanes, before re-correcting and getting back on track.

Deep breaths.

Gripping the steering wheel tighter, he stamped the accelerator once more and shot forward, passing a sign which indicated Memorial Bridge just ahead, meaning Capitol City lay just a few miles away.

If the autonomous system had failed, that could only mean the satellite network had failed.

Impossible!

He, himself, had made sure there were redundancies and safety precautions built in to ensure a signal would never fail. And it hadn't, well, until now. He'd need to have Solomon look into this, but first he needed to survive the remainder of his drive.

He hit the override button once more, switching back to driver-less mode, to see if the signal had been recovered. The alarm sounded again and the entire dash and display flashed red.

Okay, then, manual it is, he thought as the red glow became a blue-green shimmer again.

Tightening his grip on the steering wheel, he accelerated into a curve, which brought him in view of the bridge.

The welcome sprawl of Capitol City appeared before him, beyond the bridge. It was a lovely sight to his eyes, knowing he was so close to home. In a split second he noticed the vehicles down below

The Rogue Code

haphazard in their motion, not the smooth flow of traffic he was used to seeing.

A flash of red snapped his focus back to the road ahead.

His slammed both feet on the brakes as he avoided yet another car, and came screeching to a halt just inches before slamming into the wall of stopped cars that he met as he drove onto the bridge.

The driver of the car behind him and to the right had slower reflexes. He heard the screech of tires, then the sickening crunch as it struck his car. Tremain jerked to his right, the seatbelt straining to hold his weight.

His car swung around a full 180 degrees, slamming into the guard rail on the edge of the span. In direct contradiction to its intended purpose, the guardrail snapped off and spun into the air as his car's momentum pushed through. His teeth chattered as the right two wheels slid off the roadway, feeling as well as hearing the screech of protesting metal on pavement. He gasped as he felt the car teeter.

Another car smashed into his, pushed by another collision.

There was nothing he could do.

The car slid, scraped over the edge, and fell.

Tremain had only time for one thought as he felt himself go weightless for a moment.

He scrambled for his tablet, which currently sat rolled up in his pocket.

Unfurling it, he pushed the first icon he saw.

Just as treetops crashed through the back windscreen, a coruscating light filled the cabin.

Tremain didn't hear the sickening crunch of the car's impact as he found himself face up on the lab floor, hanging half out of his matter transmitter. He breathed a sigh of relief, stood, and began brushing himself off.

"Uncle Tremain!" He heard as Christopher rushed to him.

"I'm fine, Christopher," he said as he waved his nephew off, "although I'll have some explaining to do to the rental company."

"What happened?"

"I'd like to know that myself. Solomon?"

"Welcome back, Tremain," the voice of the AI emanated from the speakers built into the lab walls, "I trust your vacation was relaxing?"

"It was. The ride home, however, we can say with absolute certainty was something else. Can you tell me what happened to the autonomous vehicle system?"

The Rogue Code

"It is offline."

Tremain rolled his eyes.

"Thank you. It's a wonder I hadn't noticed. Since when did snark enter your programming?"

"Humor is one way humans converse with each other, I have endeavored to make myself more humorous."

"In normal circumstances, I would agree with that, but we will need to have a conversation about appropriateness, don't you think?"

"Noted."

"Now, what in hell happened with the AVS?"

"I cannot access any of the systems as they are currently down. I will continue to try."

"Please do," Tremain turned to Christopher, "the car just lost the satellite signal. Lost it!"

"Is that even possible?" Christopher asked.

"Yesterday I would have laughed at the idea, but something obviously happened to it."

The lab doors slammed open. Senator Markus stormed in, panic written all over his face.

"Tremain! Thank the Gods, you're back," Markus held his hands to his chest and took several deep breaths. "The AVS system has crashed!"

"I'm well aware of that."

Markus took a seat and wrung his hands

together. He snapped his eyes to his friend as a sudden thought hit him.

"Did you just get back?" he asked.

Tremain's thin smile showed the strain he had just endured.

"Yes. Just. Like a few seconds ago."

Markus frowned, nodded, and resumed his hand-wringing.

"Oh, this is the worst disaster in Colony history! And just as Colony Days is starting!"

"How bad is it?" Tremain asked gently.

"Initial reports have us at hundreds injured, but thankfully, only one death so far. A car tumbled off Memorial Bridge just a short while ago. Poor chap. I hope he didn't suffer."

Tremain cleared his throat and raised his hand.

"That chap was me. Thanks to my transmitter, I'm here instead of impaled on a tree."

"Ah, yes, well," Markus looked at Tremain, his eyes wide, "Quite fortunate, that. Looks like you got some sun."

Tremain clapped his hands together.

"Well, I have Solomon looking into the cause of the failure, so we can make sure it never happens again," he paused, and looked sideways at Markus, "wait, you said Colony Days is starting? I thought it started tomorrow ..."

"Nope," Christopher spoke up, glancing up from his tablet, "the symposium you wanted to see is tonight. Celeste and I are going too, we get extra credit if we write up a summary for social studies class."

"That's tonight?" Tremain moaned, and spread his hands in frustration, "All my appropriate clothes were in that car, I have nothing to wear!"

Christopher shook his head and smiled.

"I'm sure my dad has something you can wear for now, we can go shopping for you tomorrow."

"I'm sure your father has lots of things in his closet, but also remember your father favored the dreaded jumpsuit era of the early colonists," Tremain rolled his eyes and gave a mock shudder, "There's more burnt orange in that man's wardrobe than should be legally allowed, so I don't quite trust your father's dress sense." He grimaced once more at the thought and then threw a wink at his nephew, "I'll just have to dust off that old suit I have sitting around and meet you later." He paused and considered something. "Extra credit you say? Like you need it."

"Well, when Lyda Stryker gives a talk, they want to make sure we're paying attention."

Markus turned to Christopher, the question clear on his face.

"Lyda Stryker runs the biggest tech company in the colonies," Christopher said as he held up his smart tablet, now firmly wrapped around his wrist, "we wouldn't have the fun things we have today if not for her work, plus almost everyone uses her apps, from security to games. I've just downloaded her new productivity game, it's pretty cool."

"Oh, I know who she is," Markus protested, "I just rarely use my tablet. Guess that makes me out of touch."

"No, Markus," Tremain interjected, putting an arm around his friend's shoulder, "that just makes you a busy senator. I'm sure you'll get around to playing games."

Markus stood, a resigned look on his face.

"Well, I have to face the news media now. I'm sure they're swarming all over the senatorial offices, looking for whatever story they can dig up."

"Go on, then. Charm them as usual."

"I have no idea how I'm going to present the news, this is tragic."

"Off like a bandage, I always say," Tremain joked,

The Rogue Code

"Give them the bad news and say we're working on the cause. Then mutter 'no comment' when they want more details," Tremain laughed, "I should have been a senator, no, check that, I'd be bored silly."

Markus gave a sad grin, shook his head, waved, and left the lab.

Desmond shuffled over to Christopher, leaning on his ever-present broom.

"Go on yourselves, get ready for your fancy talk. I'll lock it all up here." He turned his sharp gaze to Tremain, "Think we've all had enough excitement for one day?"

Tremain clapped his hands together and nodded.

"Yes, I believe I agree with that sentiment."

Christopher grabbed his backpack and left. Tremain stayed behind, staring at his transmitter.

"What's on your mind?" Desmond asked.

"This talk tonight: Technology and its effect on Society, or whatever they've called it. I have my own technology to thank for saving my life today. I'd say that's a pretty good record to run on, don't you?"

Desmond looked at his long-time coworker and friend.

"Yeah, but you'd still make a horrible senator." He laughed, "Oh, before I forget, some kid has been calling. Third time today ... he keeps saying he has something important he needs to talk to you about, but didn't leave a number or any way to get back to him." Desmond scratched his head, "sounded serious."

"If he follows his apparent pattern, I'm sure he'll call back. I suppose I should hear what he has to say, even if it is a prank."

Desmond acknowledged with a nod, and went about shutting things down for the night.

Tremain watched his friend for a moment, then smiled, put his hands in his pockets, and left the lab.

2

The light breeze drifted over Christopher and Celeste as they walked, hand in hand, to the University Auditorium.

"I hope you don't get bored by this." Christopher said as they rounded a corner. The auditorium was in sight now, only a few blocks further.

"I won't," Celeste answered as she gave his hand a squeeze, "I'll have you there."

Christopher grinned.

"Besides, it's always good to feed our heads. Or as Uncle Tremain likes to call it, our 'big squishy thing'."

Celeste laughed.

"What?" She stopped and put her hands to her mouth, "Why does he call a brain that?"

"You haven't heard his theory of evolution, have you?"

Celeste shook her head, a quizzical look on her face.

"No, I haven't. Please, do tell."

Christopher grabbed the imaginary lapels of a lab coat and cleared his throat.

"We are basically a conglomeration of squishy things, or for short, CSTs. Each thing came to be to perform some sort of function in the provision of input, nutrition, or locomotion to the great big squishy thing which resides comfortably in its bone armor," at this, Christopher pointed both index fingers at his skull, "without which, we wouldn't be who we are, and without all the other squishy things, our one big squishy thing would be sedentary and become quite bored."

Christopher nodded his head in a perfect imitation of his uncle as he finished. Celeste laughed again.

"Tremain can be so weird sometimes."

"Yes, he can be. But he's pretty cool too. I wonder if he dusted off that suit?"

They'd reached the front doors of the auditorium by now and pushed their way through the crowd to the speaking hall. Christopher saw a portly boy wearing a plaid shirt with glasses perched low on his nose waving at them.

"There's Squeaks. He was going to save seats for us." Christopher said as he waved back.

"Why do you call him Squeaks?" Celeste asked.

"Because when he gets laughing, he starts to squeak. We've called him that since grade school."

Celeste shook her head, all but exasperated at boys and their nicknames.

Christopher found their seats and made introductions.

"Guys, this is Celeste."

A young, thin man with a thick head of black hair sitting just in front of Squeaks pushed an ever-present lock of hair out of his eyes and gave a low whistle.

"Knock it off, Tenny." Christopher glared at his friend.

"I came for the wrong attraction," Tenny whispered, and offered his hand, "Name's Tennyson. Everyone just calls me Tenny."

"Tennyson like the poet?" Celeste asked as she shook hands.

"You know it!" Tenny grinned and gave a mock salute.

Christopher rolled his eyes and indicated the portly boy again.

"This is Squeaks, and next to him is Zach." The small, quiet boy with his blond hair brushed back, looked up from his tablet and gave a double take. He visibly swallowed before waving hello, then went back to his tablet.

Squeaks had his own tablet in hand, waving it toward Christopher.

"Did you see the new app?" he asked.

Christopher nodded his head.

"Yes, but I haven't had time to get really into it yet."

"It's pretty cool. Supposed to increase critical thinking and fine tune reflexes. I don't know about that, but it's fun to play with."

"Found it!" Zach exclaimed, clapping his hands and showing his tablet screen to his friends.

"Found what?" Celeste asked Christopher.

Zach pointed out a symbol on the screen.

"The guy who writes most of the code for these apps usually puts his signature in each one, and there's a contest to see who can find it first. See it?"

Celeste leaned over Christopher to check it out. Zach's finger indicated a strange symbol; typed characters in varying shapes and sizes twisted and intertwined to create a familiar shape.

"It looks like a dinosaur?" She asked.

Zach nodded, smiling.

"Zach usually finds it before anyone else," Christopher said, "They've asked him to wait at least a week before calling it in, just to give others a chance."

They all laughed as Zach shrugged and they all sat back in their seats.

"I can't help it that I'm just that good!" Zach said.

Christopher turned to Celeste.

"We're all in computer class together. We'll get extra credit for this talk in there too."

Celeste nodded, then gave Christopher a side-eye look.

"And what do I get?" she asked, a half-smile on her face.

"Hopefully a fun time, and my gratitude."

"I was hoping for a kiss."

Squeaks let out a low moan.

"Could you two be any more nauseating?" he pointed toward the stage, "Look, it's about to start now."

The house lights dimmed and a spotlight illuminated a man walking onto the stage.

"Ladies and gentlemen, I'm Maddix Kirk, president of events here at the university. I can't tell you how excited I am to kick off our Colony Days celebration with this talk tonight on Technology and Society. We have for you, direct from her campus, Lyda Stryker!"

Hands clapped and the audience stood as a woman walked on stage from the opposite side. She waved toward the crowd and shook hands with Kirk. She stood about the same height as the events president. Her slacks and black turtleneck complemented her dark skin and short cropped black hair. The only extra adornment she wore was a small golden locket around her neck. Christopher could see a headpiece microphone wrapped around her ear, the mike hitting just at the corner of her mouth.

Kirk made his exit, the spotlight now illuminating Stryker.

"Welcome!" she said through the applause, her voice betraying just a hint of an accent, "As you may know, I am the owner and president of Stryker Technologies." More applause. She waved her hands to quiet the crowd, "Our latest app, released just a few short days ago, has been downloaded by over 75 percent of the active devices in the colonies. In short, you've made us the most popular app developer in colony history."

The crowd erupted in applause once again. Stryker stood and let it wash over her.

"Now, you may think that's a wonderful achievement, and it is, but what does that say about us as a society?" she let the question hang in the air for a moment, "Just before I came on stage, I watched you in the audience. Many of you had your heads bowed, looking at your devices instead of conversing with the people next to you."

Christopher looked around, noticing that most of the people in his line of sight were students like him and his friends, with a few Professors and other adults mixed in. He recognized a few students from his social studies class, they were probably starting their reports. His brow furrowed as he wondered what point she was trying to make.

"Look around on a daily basis and what do you see? People with their heads down, looking at their devices instead of the world around them. Students, like many of you, who prefer to talk via a device rather than face-to-face," Her gaze roamed over the crowd, "We, as a society, are becoming more and more disconnected, even as we become more connected through our devices. Which is why I can stand here this evening and say, with full conviction, that our rampant use of technology is a problem. It's become an evil and must be stopped."

Christopher heard gasps around him, the loudest coming from his right. He turned to see his uncle Tremain, sitting across the aisle and a row back, arms folded in indignation as he shook his head. Tremain had indeed dug out his old suit, Christopher saw he hadn't quite brushed out the dust that had settled on the shoulders. He turned his attention back to the stage.

Stryker held her hands up, calming the crowd.

"I know what you're thinking. I've been called the technology queen, the wizard of the app world. How can I proclaim such a radical thing? It's because I care more about the society I live in, than what game is the most popular," She reached into her back pocket and pulled out an index card, waving it towards the audience, "Let me share some stats with you:

"As our technology has improved, we've seen fewer families who actually eat a meal together. We've seen more instances of depression, especially among our youngest citizens. Our social media profiles are more important to us than the number of actual physical friends we interact with. We live our lives through our networks, not by actively living them. Not only that, but with all our smart devices, all the information at our fingertips as well as any surface that has a smart film applied, we've become more isolated. We don't need to see a doctor as our devices monitor our health for us. They learn our habits, so in effect, they know what we want before we know it ourselves. We're becoming more obese as we become more sedentary. Our children pay attention to their social media more than to their parents. Teenagers have a technology mania, or fever, or dare I say it, lust."

There were more gasps from the audience.

"Incendiary allegations, I'm well aware," Lyda continued, "but I fear we're seeing the crumbling of our society due to these things." She waved a tablet in the air, the thin film reflecting the spotlight. She crumbled it in her hands, destroying it. "I believe our technology isn't the boon to our society as we thought it would be. It's become the harbinger of our end."

Christopher flinched when he heard his uncle shout.

"Ridiculous!"

Stryker's head swiveled around at the exclamation. She gave a double take as she did so.

"Oh no." Christopher moaned as he shrunk back into his seat. Celeste gave him a quizzical look. On stage, Stryker waved her hand towards the spot where Tremain sat.

"Ladies and gentlemen, we have a celebrity in the audience. Professor Tremain!" she gestured towards the stage, "Please, Professor, join me onstage. I'd love to hear your opinions on this. We can have a debate."

Squeaks turned to Christopher, a glint in his eye.

"Five bucks says your uncle wipes the stage with her."

Christopher stared in amazement at Squeaks as Tenny giggled from the seat in front.

"Oh this is gonna be good!" Tenny squealed and rubbed his hands together.

Tremain stood as applause filled the auditorium. His rumpled sport jacket covered a shirt and tie instead of the normal lab coat and he looked quite dapper, apart from the dust on the shoulders and the indignant glare on his face. He marched over to the stage stairs as a tech brought out a pair of chairs and another headset for the scientist.

Tremain sat, adjusted the microphone and cleared his throat.

"Now just what are you getting on about? Technology lust? Really!" he sputtered as the mic activated.

Stryker smiled at the scientist, exuding confidence.

"I describe what I witness."

"You really need to study history too. Every generation has its own thing, would you believe the exact same terms were used in the 18th century on Earth in regards to another great technological feat?" Tremain glanced around the audience, "Can you guess what it was?"

"Enlighten me, Professor." Stryker said as she folded her arms.

"The printing press. Books. They were widely available for the first time. Now knowledge was able to be widely disseminated. There were arguments about people getting ideas. That they'd fill their heads with so much garbage. That people would choose to read instead of working the land and society would break down. Sound familiar?"

There came sporadic applause from the crowd as Stryker glanced at them.

"Insidious things, books," Tremain continued, "They did get some people thinking, though. Because of books, because of those ideas, our ancestors created things like calculus, automobiles, space flight, Formica ... well, maybe that last one wasn't quite up to par, but my point is you never know where inspiration will come from. Maybe one of these students in the audience will create the next greatest thing that will forever change how we live our lives?"

More applause from the crowd. Stryker's brows furrowed as she waved her hands in front of her, conceding a point to Tremain.

"How many deaths were there from those inventions?" she asked. The crowd died down. "How many automobile accidents, how many people lost their lives in space flight? With every technological marvel, there is an increase in injuries and deaths. Look at today's fiasco with the autonomous vehicle system. You say this is all a good thing, but lives were at stake today. Is it really worth it?"

It was Tremain's turn to frown.

"Progress isn't always as neat and clean as we'd like. You are only focusing on the negative aspects of progress. Today's malfunction, and I was caught up in it myself, is being investigated as we speak. I have no doubt we'll get to the bottom of it and prevent further issues to boot. But aside from that, let's talk about all the lives saved by technology. Medical technology has improved by leaps and bounds. How many illnesses are found early due to medical smart screening technology? How many lives have been saved due to vaccines that were discovered? Look back through the records of the past and you'll see how the death rates plummeted after certain vaccines were invented. Would you have us go back that far? Education has improved since we've installed smart films to almost every surface. Surely, you don't believe those are evil? You say you want to abolish technology. Where do you draw that line? Eating utensils and fire were once considered high technology. Shall we go back to the stone age?"

In the audience, Zach handed a five-dollar bill to Squeaks. Tenny turned around.

"It's not over yet," he whispered, and turned back to face the stage.

Christopher watched as Stryker stood and paced the stage in obvious agitation.

"Surely, we can agree that our society is more isolated than ever before due to technology?" she asked.

Tremain sighed.

"Technology is only a tool. Like any tool, it has a designed use. Consider a hammer, another tool that was once also considered a time-saving bit of technology. Do you blame the hammer if it's used to hurt another person or do you blame the user? Our technology is the same. It's not the fault of technology if issues arise, rather, it's the fault of the user," he held his hands up in the air, "besides, the cat is out of the bag, the genie has left its bottle, Pandora's box is opened. You can't stop progress." He shrugged.

"And what if we had an opportunity to close Pandora's Box?" Stryker asked, her eyes alight, "What then?"

Tremain sat for a few seconds in total silence. The crowd became uneasy. Christopher shifted in his seat. Celeste's attention never wavered from the drama unfolding onstage.

"You know, this makes me think of a sobering fact: scientists have realized, through science, and yes, technology, that there are around 12 million stars born every day in our galaxy alone." Tremain finally said.

"I don't see the point."

Tremain held up a finger and bowed his head.

"Considering all things, if only ten percent of those stars developed planets, if only ten percent of those planets were far enough away from their star to have liquid water, if only ten percent of those planets developed some sort of life, we'd have at least 120,000 worlds teeming with life. If of those life-generating planets, only 10 percent of 10 percent of 10 percent of those planets developed a higher from of life, sentient, intelligent, capable of looking up in wonder, just think of the possibilities."

"And?" Stryker asked, arms crossed, tapping her foot.

"Don't you see how rare intelligent life is in the universe? Do we even know how we would identify an intelligent life form? We scientists think we do, and then I have a conversation like this one today and I wonder if we've not set that bar far too low."

The audience erupted in cheers and applause. Tenny turned to Squeaks and slapped a 5 dollar bill into his hands, shaking his head, a wry smile on his face.

On stage, Lyda Stryker's face darkened, her rage barely contained just below the surface. She glared at Tremain for a second or two before visibly releasing tension. A smile spread across her face as she turned back to the audience.

"That was quite an opinion! I think that's all the time I have today, thank you for coming!"

She ripped the headset off her brow, dropped it to the floor, and stalked off the stage, leaving Tremain standing alone, hand outstretched. Maddix Kirk rushed out to shake Tremain's hand and thank him, as the crowd began to filter out of the auditorium.

Outside, in an alleyway behind the building, a black car waited, its electric engine humming. Inside, Lyda Stryker fumed. The nerve of that man embarrassing her like that. Couldn't he see she had the higher moral argument? Her hand instinctively went to the locket around her neck. She caressed it between her thumb and forefinger as she fumed. Finally controlling her anger, she thumbed a button on her smart film wrist wrap.

"Yes, ma'am?" came the man's voice on the other end of the connection.

"Our timetable has changed. We're moving up phase two."

"Very well, ma'am. I'll inform the staff."

Stryker sat back and took a deep breath. She motioned her driver to get going, crossed her arms as the car began moving, entering the all but deserted streets. A dark smile spread across her features.

Soon...

3

New Earth Today interview
Hawking labs

"This is Ellie Travers coming to you live today from Hawking labs. I have the honor to have as my guest Professor Tremain." The blond, bright-eyed reporter turned her wide smile to Tremain, who shifted uncomfortably in his chair. They'd set up the video on the top floor of the cafeteria, clearing out the floor for privacy. Not that there were many people to usher out as it was early in the morning. Still, the air was full of the sweet smells of the flowering plants in the center part of the atrium. The botanists had done a great job.

Tremain cleared his throat, his nerves were getting the better of him. He agreed to do the interview at the request of Senator Markus, his friend. After the incidents with the rifts, caused by Marjorie messing with unprotected, unshielded lodestones, which the public could not help but notice, Hawking labs had been hit with some bad press. Getting out in front of it was important, Markus had explained. Tremain agreed, even if he didn't like it. He cleared his throat once more, the microphone clipped to his lab coat lapel, picking up everything clearly.

"My pleasure, Ellie."

"For a lab that has made such contributions to the colonies, I was very surprised I didn't know much about what you do here. I had to do some research."

Tremain smiled.

"Well, we do tend to keep a low profile."

"Low profile? Excuse me, but the rifts were not low profile."

Tremain held his hands up as if to say: calm down.

"That wasn't us. We did discover what was causing them, and put a stop to it."

"What caused them?"

"I'm afraid I can't tell you. It's classified."

"Is there a lot of classified research that happens in this building?"

"Buildings, actually. This one we're in now is the largest, with wings for the history departments, the archeology and botany departments, etc. We have separate labs for other projects, some public, and some secret."

"Secret labs? Classified research? Sounds mysterious."

"Oh, not really," Tremain waved a hand, "some research we do is military in nature, or we're pushing the envelope, so we tend to keep those under wraps until we know where we're heading. Our main contributions to society have started the same way."

"I see," Ellie said, pushing a lock of hair behind her ear, and smiling sweetly with a slight head tilt. That usually tended to disarm her male interviewees, freeing up their tongues just a little bit more. "I've looked up what you have had a hand in yourself, as far as contributions go." She consulted her tablet, "It's a long list with the train system and the driver-less car system to name just two." She looked up from her tablet, her brows knitting together, "How serious was the problem yesterday with the autonomous car system? What happened?"

Tremain shifted once again.

"Yes, I happened to get caught up in that myself. We're still investigating, but I'm confident we'll have answers as to what exactly happened soon."

"So a day later and you still don't know?" Ellie asked, concern etched in her face.

"I didn't say that. Somehow, all our redundant systems for safety failed. Like I said, we're investigating just how that occurred, and will make sure it can't happen again."

"Is your new AI working on that with you?" She asked with a gotcha look on her face.

Tremain looked puzzled for a moment. But of course that information had to have gotten out after his rather blustery performance in front of the Senate council a few months ago. He nodded slightly and smiled.

"Solomon has become quite the useful addition to the lab staff. I'm hoping he can grow to become a productive member of the colony. Yes, he is helping us with our investigation."

The Rogue Code

"Aren't there some concerns with giving an AI such access to sensitive systems like that?"

Tremain shook his head.

"Oh I wouldn't worry too much about that. I trust Solomon to do his job as much as I'd trust any one of my staff."

"But we've all read stories of a rogue AI taking over the world …"

Tremain cut her off.

"They're just stories. Sensational and quite fictional stories too. Stories like that sell. Reality is much more sedate, thankfully. Solomon has no designs to take over humanity. He prefers to help. Think of him as a puppy. A very intelligent puppy, but a puppy nonetheless."

Ellie laughed at the comparison.

"So, how does your puppy help out at the lab? Does he conduct research or experiments?"

"No, nothing like that. He monitors our systems and controls security around the lab complex. He's very good at keeping watch, and there have been no accidents or issues since he's been added to the staff."

"That's good to hear, Professor. Now," she shifted and adopted a more serious look on her face, "I wouldn't be a very good interviewer if I didn't touch on your confrontation with Lyda Stryker last night."

Tremain rolled his eyes.

"Don't get me started." He said.

"I know, technology as an evil?" She waved her hands to indicate the video cameras and her tablet, "I couldn't do my job without it. What could she have been thinking?"

"That's just it. What was she thinking? Oh, everyone is entitled to their own opinions, I'm frankly quite embarrassed that I didn't dig deeper."

Ellie knitted her brows and smiled slightly.

"I think you won the argument, wouldn't you agree?"

"The argument wasn't the point. Winning it isn't the point. It was the fact that she posited a position that was opposite of my own. Instead of trying to understand why she held such an opinion, I dismissed it and her outright. Shameful, if you ask me."

Ellie sat back, surprised.

"You're saying you'd rather try to understand a frankly crazy opinion instead of shoving it away outright?"

"Exactly. How do you think science and research work? Any idea is a good one until a better one comes along, no matter how out-there it may be."

"Do you think it's possible?"

"What do you mean?" Tremain asked.

"To put the genie back in the bottle?"

"To regress, you mean?" Tremain laughed, "No, I rather think that's a pipe dream. Progress can't be stopped. Not really. Eventually, someone will take a step forward, push a boundary, so to speak, and that pulls everything else with it."

"So what's next for Hawking and your lab in particular?"

Tremain thought for a moment.

"We have some projects in the works, not that I can talk about any of them yet, but rest assured, we're making progress." He smiled, emphasizing the last word.

Ellie smiled back at him.

"I read you loud and clear, Professor." She reached out a hand, which Tremain shook, "I thank you for allowing us to take up some of your valuable time. It's been a pleasure."

"Mine as well. Call anytime."

The lights cut out, and the smile on Ellie Travers' face faded as the camera stopped rolling. She gathered up her things, ignoring Tremain. Her tablet vibrated and she walked off towards the stairs, nose buried in her device.

Tremain watched, amused. Maybe Lyda Stryker did have a point. The cameramen and sound engineers packed up their equipment and filed out of the atrium. He sat alone for a few moments, enjoying the silence.

4

Christopher made his way to his coding class, his mind in a whirl. He pushed past the bustle of the other students, barely noticing them as he walked.

He couldn't keep his mind off of the explosive talk from last night. How could such a successful person want to get rid of the very thing that made them successful in the first place?

He couldn't fathom it at all.

He turned the corner into the coding class, pausing just moment for another student to hurry in just ahead of him.

"New Earth to Christopher ..." He heard as a murmur in the background as he sat down. He blinked his eyes to see Tenny, Squeaks, and Zach all staring at him.

"What?"

Squeaks let out his high-pitched squeaking laugh.

"You were somewhere else, man. Celeste give you one heck of a kiss or what?" Which prompted giggles and back-pats from the other two. Christopher shrugged it off.

"No, nothing like that. I can't help but think about last night."

Tenny sat back in his chair and clasped his hands behind his head.

"So, it wasn't just a kiss, was it?" He laughed, "Come on, Chris, give us the goods ..."

Christopher glared at him.

"I meant the speech."

Squeaks nodded his head and gave an emphatic fist-pump.

"If words were weapons, Lyda Stryker would be as good as buried. Your uncle wiped the stage with her!" he shook his head with the memory, a smile on his face.

Before any further discussion could happen, the professor walked in. His thin, wiry hair looked like he'd just jumped out of bed. His pants were just a bit too short and his cardigan, which once could have been some sort of green color, now seemed more dingy blah than anything else. His eyes swept the room. He cleared his throat and was just about to speak when the lights flickered.

They flared once, went out, and then came back on.

Each smart film screen, one by one, popped up with a blue screen of death. The entire class broke out in groans.

The professor, not saying a word, walked over to the wall, opened a cabinet and flicked a switch. Immediately, each computer rebooted, only to show a blank, blue screen once again.

"Well, that's never happened before." He said to himself, scratched his head, then flicked the switch again.

At the same moment, the lights in the room all flickered off again. The clock image on the smart wall warped, the digital hands on the analog face spun, flickered, and the whole wall went blank. The lights came on once more, then, with a flash and a fizzle, they went out again. In fact, everything went out.

Every smart screen in the room faded to a

pinpoint of blue, then went out. No lights, no sounds but the students' breathing ... nothing.

Christopher gave a wary eye to Tenny, who held his hands up in a 'who me' gesture. Squeaks shook his head and looked to Zach who just looked around and mouthed 'wasn't me'.

One of the secretaries from the office opened the door, breathless, as she stuck her head in and all but shouted;

"Students are to exit the school quickly and orderly. Classes have been canceled for the day!"

The class erupted in half cheers, half groans, but they all filed out, Christopher hung back with his friends.

"Something isn't right about this. If none of you did this, who did?"

Tenny smiled.

"Does it matter? Whoever it was just did us a huge favor. No English class today!" and he gave a war whoop.

Christopher hit him in the arm.

"Knock it off, Tenny. Something is up. Let me grab Celeste and let's meet at the lab."

Squeaks shrugged.

"Sure, Chris. It's not like we have anything else to do now."

Zach nodded and they promised to meet back in a half-hour.

Christopher rushed up the stairs and met Celeste at her locker.

"Hey Christopher!" she said, smiling as she placed a textbook in her backpack. "Which one of them did it?"

Christopher blinked for a moment, then he realized what she was asking.

"Oh, no, it wasn't them. I have no idea who did this. But I'm going to try and figure it out. Want to come to the lab?"

Celeste put her hand on her heart and mock-fainted into her locker.

"Oh, you ask me on the most romantic dates." Then she giggled and slammed her locker shut, "I said I was up for more adventure, didn't I? I have a feeling this will fit the bill."

Christopher smiled.

"Well, come on, then!"

A HALF-HOUR LATER, they all met at the lab, where they proceeded to give Tremain and Desmond the rundown of the morning's events.

Tremain scratched his head.

"So you say they all went out?" he called up to the ceiling, "Solomon, what can you tell me about it?"

Solomon's ever-more-human sounding voice came through the speakers.

"I do not have access to those systems as they are secured, however, I do notice the security is down at the moment." He paused, "Yes, it is indeed down. Shall I ask the school server?"

Tremain rolled his eyes.

"Yes, of course!" He looked at the teenagers grouped in front of him, "As intuitive as he is, sometimes ..."

"The server, as well as everything else at the school, is down." Solomon said, as calm as can be, "I cannot gain access to it at the moment."

"Keep trying," Tremain said, "and let me know if you find anything."

"Certainly."

Tremain rubbed his chin.

"OK, so yesterday, we had the autonomous car system break down. Solomon discovered the satellites were all functioning perfectly, so the AVS system itself is at fault. I'm currently assuming a virus. Today, it's the school." He sat down heavily at his desk, "I'm still no closer to figuring yesterday out, and then there's that talk last night. I feel a little sheepish."

"You did great!" Zach said.

"She's an idiot to think she could out-smart you." Squeaks added.

Tremain waved them all off.

"Like I said this morning during my interview, what I didn't do was listen. I was so shocked by Lyda Stryker's exclamation that I just reacted."

"Yeah, but she was wrong." Tenny broke in.

Tremain shook his head.

"The first rule in any conversation is to listen and try to understand the other's point of view. I didn't do that, I only beat down her argument without even an attempt at understanding." He stood and shrugged, "So, I think I owe her an apology."

Christopher nodded, he knew his uncle well enough to know when he'd made his mind up.

"Are you going to call her?"

"This kind of apology deserves a face to face. I'm going to run over there to her office and see if she'll meet with me. It's the least I can do," He looked at each of them, "And what will you all be doing? I'm assuming homework is not on the agenda?"

"If Solomon can get into the school system, we're

going to see if we can track who hacked into it." Christopher said.

Tremain nodded.

"Very good. Maybe you all can help me with the auto system too. It's back up and running, but searching through the code is like looking for a needle in a haystack."

The teenagers all agreed to help and Tremain left. Celeste sat down at the desk. Desmond gestured to them to follow him.

"If you all are going to get to searching, you'll need some space, come on." He led them out of the lab to an unused office. He shuffled a few boxes out of the way and turned on the lights. A smart wall flickered to life. "Tremain set this space aside for some project or other, but it just became storage. Might as well get some good use out of it." He gestured to the desk that was half-buried in boxes and files, "There's a terminal over there too, so you should be able to work in groups." He shuffled out the door, "call me if you need me!"

Tenny sniffed, looking at the clutter.

"It's better than doing homework, that's for sure."

Zach picked up a small pile of folders.

"Were should we move all this stuff?"

The Rogue Code

Christopher gave the room a once-over and then pointed to the far wall.

"Might as well stack it over there," he glanced towards the ceiling, "Solomon, are you in here?"

The synthesized voice answered, loud and clear.

"I would say I was everywhere if that didn't sound so ... pompous."

Christopher grinned. Solomon's personality was evolving by the day.

"Great. Are any of these smart walls?"

In response, the walls on either side of the doorway wall glowed to life.

"What would you like to display?"

Christopher gave a glance over to the dusty terminal.

"How about a look at the code from the autonomous car system? We can look for anything that might give us a clue."

"There are many million lines of code. I've been through it many times since yesterday and cannot find any erroneous code."

Discouraged, Christopher scratched his head, unconsciously aping his uncle's gesture.

"Not that I think you missed anything, but maybe we can have a look too."

"Of course. I'll put it on both walls, so you can analyze it faster."

The glowing walls changed, no longer showing the standard off-white, but now were filling with lines and lines of code. Tenny looked up at all the characters, giving a low whistle.

"Looks like we have our work cut out for us."

Celeste frowned as the seemingly arcane series of characters and symbols filled her vision. She shook her head.

"What can I do to help? I have no idea what I'm looking for in this gobbledygook." She gestured towards the walls.

Christopher thought for a moment, then an idea came to him.

"Solomon, did you check all the code? Even the comment codes?"

Celeste frowned again.

"Comment codes?"

Squeaks nodded his head.

"Yeah, sometimes a programmer writes notes to himself, but he uses a specific character set to separate it from the actual program code. It's called a comment code. Doesn't affect anything."

"Oh," Celeste answered, "so, you think maybe the virus would be in a comment?"

Solomon's voice crackled over the speakers.

"I did not analyze the comment codes, only the program coding."

Christopher pointed towards Celeste.

"And that's where you'll start."

Celeste looked confused.

"And how will I know what I'm looking for?"

Zach pulled up a chair next to Celeste and brushed off the dust, causing them all to start coughing.

"I'll help you. It'll be fun." He smiled.

Celeste sighed.

Fun.

5

Tremain stood across the plaza from the main Stryker Technology building. The campus consisted of a series of buildings about ten miles up the coast from the lab. Employees strolled the landscaped pathways between the buildings, coffee cups in hand. Each building, from what Tremain could see, had many windows, the better to let in as much natural light as possible. Tremain grinned. It was rare that he actually went outside himself, he could only imagine what even more introverted programmers were like. He turned his attention back to the task at hand.

A free-standing sign, containing the company logo, a stylized S fading into ones and zeroes with the company name *"Stryker Technologies* "glowing underneath, sprawled to the side of a glass doorway, well-manicured bushes and shrubs planted around it.

She probably won't even speak to me. I wouldn't blame her, either.

He paced around the small fountain in the center of the plaza, sunlight glinting off the coins that had been tossed into the bottom, his thoughts vacillating between whether Lyda Stryker would spurn his apologies or if she'd listen and they'd have a nice conversation.

Taking a deep breath, Tremain took the final few steps to the door and entered.

The enormous lobby seemed very welcoming. Plush couches and chairs were grouped in clusters around the large room, area rugs underneath. Some workers were taking meetings, bathed in the sunlight, their tablets or actual papers scattered on the coffee tables before them. Beyond the cozy furniture stood a long desk, where numerous receptionists stood or sat. The familiar scent of roasted coffee beans brought Tremain's attention to a coffee bar set up at one end of the lobby. The heady aroma made the lobby seem all that more cozy, more like a coffee shop than a tech company. Tremain made his way to one of the receptionists.

"May I help you sir?" She said in a tiny voice. She seemed young, not much older than Christopher. Her bright red hair pulled back into a crisp ponytail lent her a severe look.

"Yes, I'm here to see Lyda Stryker."

The girl paused only a moment, blinking rapidly.

"She's very busy sir. Would you care to leave a message? I'll be sure she gets it."

"Tell her it's Tremain and I'm here to apologize."

The girl blinked a few more times. Tremain was starting to wonder if she wasn't an advanced android and was about to take a peek over the desk when she tapped her ear and began speaking.

"Yes Ms. Stryker, a mister Tremain to see you." She blinked, nodded curtly and tapped her ear once more. Her gaze fell on Tremain once again and she cleared her throat. "She'll be right down to meet you."

The other receptionists stole glances at each other, movements Tremain didn't miss. What sort of CEO was Lyda Stryker if her employees were this skittish?

"Thank you. I'll just wait over here." He said as he pointed towards one of the closer plush chairs. He was about to sit down when he saw Lyda exit a corridor and turn towards the lobby.

An almost reverent hush fell. Tremain saw the groups of employees all stop what they were doing and turn towards their employer. Stryker seemed to take no notice, her gaze fixed on Tremain. A man wearing a security jumpsuit and an ear-piece intercepted her before she could move further. He said something to her in a low voice, his hands held outward at his sides, shaking his head. Her expression changed to fury.

"Find him!" she hissed loud enough for Tremain to hear. The security officer took a step back, then rushed away.

Lyda took a moment to settle herself, then pierced Tremain with her gaze once more.

"Tremain!" she called, "To what do I owe this pleasure?" She walked over to him and shook his hand, her handshake warm and firm.

Tremain stood somewhat nonplussed. This, coupled with that last exchange was not what he had expected.

"Hello, Lyda. I wasn't sure you'd agree to see me after last night."

Lyda's laugh filled the lobby, making more heads turn. She made a dismissive gesture.

"What are you talking about? I enjoyed our sparring."

"Well, that's what I'm here about. I came to apologize for my behavior."

She tilted her head, fingering a button on her immaculate shirt.

"Apologize? Whatever for?"

Tremain held his hands out.

"For starters, I dismissed your point of reasoning out of turn. I prefer to try and understand a differing point of view, but I neglected to do that last evening," he paused, "can you forgive me?"

Lyda laughed once more, a genuine laugh, and shook her head.

"Forgive you? Of course." She turned as if to go back to work, but stopped half-way and looked to him and gestured down the corridor, "Would you like to join me for a bite? Maybe we might try to convince each other of our differing viewpoints."

Tremain smiled, straightened and tucked his hands in his lab pockets.

"I'd be delighted!"

In the lab, the teenagers pored over the code, Christopher, Squeaks and Tenny analyzing the displays on the wall. Each had a section they were going over. Every once in a while, Squeaks would remove his glasses and rub his eyes.

"After a while, it all starts to blur together." He muttered.

Tenny barked out a short laugh.

"No kidding," he gave Squeaks a playful tap on the shoulder, "come on, Squeaks, we're going to save the world if we find this virus or whatever it is."

Squeaks replaced his glasses and gave a nod. Yes, they would save the world.

Over at the desk, Celeste just shook her head as she scanned the code. Zach was a decent teacher, but she still didn't know what she was looking at or for. Next to her, Zach grumbled.

"This formatting just looks funny, don't you think?" he asked

"What do you mean? Is it supposed to look a certain way?" Celeste asked, confusion clear in her voice.

"Well, yeah. There are certain conventions you follow, just like for papers in English class."

"Oh, I see." Celeste answered, still not really understanding, "So, you think this isn't formatted correctly?"

Zach pointed at the small section on the screen.

"See here? There's a comment, but it's just

garbage. No way a virus can be hiding in there," he scratched bend his ear as he scrolled down, "and here, there's just a short couple of characters in the comment. It makes no sense."

Celeste glared at the screen, as if it would reveal some secret.

"It's like it's only a small part of a bigger picture." She murmured.

Zach turned his head to her in a slow arc, his eyes getting wider as he did so.

"You. Are. A. Genius." He yelled and ran his hands over the screen, making the code shrink. He all but shook as he saw the results. "Oh no."

"What?" Celeste asked, not sure yet again what she was supposed to see.

Zach frowned.

"Solomon, can you show this on the wall for the others? Guys, you need to see this."

"Naturally, Zach." Solomon replied as Zach stood.

Christopher stepped back as the image replaced the code that was just there. He shook his head in amazement and took another step as Tenny let out a low chuckle.

"Looks like you found another one, Zach!" he folded his arms across his chest.

Christopher's spirits sank as he realized what he was seeing.

Squeaks let out a low moan.

On the wall before them, in code, was an image of a dinosaur.

6

"What does the symbol mean?" Solomon asked. Tenny explained it as fast as he could, with Zach giving commentary as he did. The room fell silent.

"What are we going to do next?" Celeste asked, "We have to let Tremain and the authorities know about this."

Squeaks pushed his glasses up his nose.

"They're not going to believe us over a symbol."

"I might be of some assistance," Solomon broke in, "A symbol or symbols similar to this were found painted on a wall in a warehouse in the industrial district a few months ago. A disturbance had been reported, but when the authorities arrived on the scene, the warehouse was empty."

Christopher frowned.

"That made the news?" he asked.

"I found an entry in a police blotter. I simply searched for symbols similar to this one."

"That warehouse could be where they worked from," Christopher said.

"Not like they were going to shoot a virus out from the Stryker campus." Tenny replied.

"Was it Stryker, though?" Celeste asked, "Are we sure? All we've found so far is garbage."

"It's the same signature," Zach answered, "it has to be the same programmer and that means he or she works for Stryker."

"Doesn't matter anyway," Squeaks chimed in, "If that hacker got into the system and left this," he gestured to the wall, "who knows what else they did. Just finding the signature shows they did something."

Celeste nodded, as she stared at the wall.

"The virus could have been a self-deleting code too, we may never find it." Tenny broke in.

"So, do we go check the warehouse out?" Zach asked.

They all turned to him, Tenny breaking into a huge grin.

"Little Zach, showing some for-ti-tude!" he

chanted.

"W-we really should let someone know ..." Squeaks piped up in a small voice.

"And tell them what, we think we found a connection?" Tenny dismissed Squeaks with a wave, "What we need to do is go check it out, like Zach suggested and see if we can find something more concrete."

Christopher, listening to it all while he glared at the symbol on the wall, whirled around.

"That's exactly what we're going to do. It's not that far, we can ride our bikes, and," he looked at Celeste, "bring your bat. Just in case."

"I thought you'd never ask." She smirked.

A WHILE LATER, they pulled up across the street from an old warehouse which, from the looks of it, had been abandoned for quite some time. The boulevard areas were all overgrown and what windows they could see were broken. Weeds had begun growing from the roof line.

Christopher stepped off his bike and raised his wrist.

"Solomon," he spoke into his smart-band, "is this the place?"

"Yes, Christopher, according to the records, you have arrived."

"Okay, keep tracking us. If there's any sign of trouble, call in the cavalry."

"I do not know how horseback soldiers will help, but I will take that to mean you are referring to the authorities."

Christopher half-smiled as he shook his head.

"Exactly, Solomon ... and thanks."

"You are welcome."

"Okay, so we just go in?" Tenny asked as he cracked his knuckles.

Christopher gave him a look as he pointed towards the far side of the warehouse.

"Tenny, you, Squeaks, and Zach go around that way, Celeste and I will go this way. If you find anything like a broken window at a height we can climb in, send a text." He waved his banded wrist.

"Sure," Tenny piped up, "Don't do anything I would." He raised his eyebrows to Celeste who shook her head and waved him off.

"Be careful." She said.

The teenagers split up, each group going their separate ways. Christopher crouched low, Celeste behind him, her baseball bat held ready.

They had just rounded the corner into an alleyway

between warehouses to find a blank wall when Christopher's wrist vibrated. He pulled up the message to read:

Would you believe we found a half-open door?

Christopher grinned and showed the text to Celeste. They ran around the building to meet the others in front of the door to find they had already started creeping in.

"HEY!" Zach's voice came from inside. Christopher heard a scuffling sound from inside, then a man's grunt.

"I got him!" Squeaks called out.

Christopher pushed his way inside to almost utter blackness. What little light that came in from the broken windows didn't go very far. Celeste turned on her flashlight and searched around by the door. Seeing a switch, she flipped it on.

The lights in the warehouse blinked into life.

Christopher immediately saw the dinosaur symbol painted on the nearest wall, in various iterations and sizes. On the cement floor before him, Squeaks had his arms wrapped around the legs of a disheveled man, with Zach sprawled across the man's chest. Tenny stood back with his hands on his knees, examining the man they'd found.

He appeared to be older than the teenagers, but

it was hard to tell how much older with the scraggly beard and long, unkempt hair. What clothes he wore, from what Christopher could see, hadn't been washed in a while.

"You're just kids!" the man exclaimed. Christopher walked over to him.

"Who are you?" he asked. Celeste stood right behind him, bat in hand.

The man gulped.

"Name's Jonas. Who are you?"

Zach jabbed the guy in the ribs.

"We're asking the questions!" he growled, causing Tenny to burst out laughing.

"Ooh, tough guy." Tenny said as he stood up straight.

"Shut up, Tenny." Christopher said as he turned back to the man, "Who did you think we were?"

"I'll tell you if you get this kid off of me."

Zach crawled off the man's chest and Squeaks slowly unwrapped the man's legs. He sat up and rubbed the back of his head.

"Thanks. I thought you guys were from ... well, I thought you were someone else."

Christopher looked around. He noticed a campstove against the wall next to which lay a sleeping bag and some old crates full of clothes and what appeared to be food.

"You're living here?"

"Hiding." The man shrugged and his hands fell limp at his sides, "not very well if you found me."

"We weren't looking for you." Christopher said and indicated the wall of symbols, "We were looking for those."

Jonas' eyes brightened and he put his hands in his pockets.

"You like 'em?" he asked, "I painted them. It's my signature."

Zach jumped like he'd been bitten.

"You're him?" he asked.

"Yeah," Jonas replied, "wait ... who do you mean?"

Christopher stopped Zach before he could say anything else.

"Zach's been finding those dinosaurs in the Stryker programs for ages. It's your signature?"

Jonas regarded Zach with new respect.

"You're the kid?" He held out his hand, "I am amazed. I tried so hard to hide those things."

"Wait," Squeaks piped in as Zach and Jonas shook hands, "this is the programmer for Stryker?" he looked Jonas up and down, unimpressed.

"Ex-programmer. I thought you guys were them coming to hunt me down."

"Why would they hunt you?" Celeste asked.

Jonas looked wary and hesitated.

"You're not going to tell them where I am?" he asked.

"We should tell the authorities." Squeaks spoke up.

Jonas shook his head.

"Oh no, don't do that. I didn't do anything."

Christopher held out a placating hand, glaring at Squeaks.

"Tell me what's going on. Why are you hiding here?"

Jonas' hands shoved deeper into his pockets.

"I used to work for Stryker. I was the top programmer there."

"And?" Christopher prodded.

"She started having us do weird stuff, like writing subroutines that didn't make sense and start hacking other closed systems. One afternoon she had me break into the auto-vehicle servers. I did, and put my signature in there, hoping someone would notice and come looking, but nothing ever happened."

"Yeah, we found that." Zach said.

Jonas nodded.

"Good. Now the authorities know."

Christopher frowned.

"We haven't told anyone yet, but that doesn't explain why you're hiding?"

"I wouldn't do it." Jonas said.

"Wouldn't do what?" Tenny prompted him.

"Hack into the military systems. I thought we were doing some other secret work before, you know, stuff above my pay grade, I didn't need to know the reason, you know? But when she started asking me to hack into the military systems, that's when I started to get worried."

"So what did you do?" Celeste asked.

"I gave her some tech speak for writing a better firewall hack, left for the day and never went back. She's up to something big."

"Okay," Tenny interjected, "you keep referring to a 'she', but we have no flipping clue who you're talking about. Who's she?"

Jonas looked at each of them in turn.

"You really haven't figured that out yet? She runs Stryker Technologies. It's Lyda Stryker."

They sat in stunned silence for a moment before Squeaks held up a hand.

"Is it just me or are you all ready to curl up into a ball?"

Tenny backhanded Squeaks' arm. Squeaks lowered his hand.

"Just me then." He whispered.

"We have to get you somewhere safe." Christopher said, "Senator Markus would know what to do."

Celeste grabbed his arm.

"But your uncle just went to go talk with her. He doesn't know what she's doing."

Christopher nodded.

"I'll message him what we've found. He's pretty capable, though, he can take care of himself."

"You ain't going anywhere." A voice called from the far end of the warehouse. They all whirled to see a man in a Stryker security jumpsuit walk out of the shadows, a large gun in his hand.

Squeaks gulped audibly.

Jonas slumped.

"How'd you find me?" he asked, his voice sounding defeated.

The man shrugged, his eyes never leaving Jonas.

"Does it matter? You knew we'd track you down sooner or later. You don't just leave, you know that."

Celeste edged away from Christopher, her eyes on the goon.

"What are you going to do with him?" Tenny asked, his usual bravado tempered.

The goon didn't move, but his eyes shifted to the teenager.

"He's coming in for a ... debriefing. You're coming too, all of you."

"What if we say no?" Tenny asked, seeing Celeste slide up to the light switch.

"That wouldn't be a very smart thing to do, now would it?" The goon said.

"Guess we're not smart!" Celeste shouted as she hit the lights.

Immediately, the warehouse went dark.

"Scatter!" Christopher yelled as a flash lit the room. The goon had fired his gun, hitting the wall where Celeste had last been.

Christopher dropped to the floor, allowing his eyes to adjust.

"Don't make it difficult for yourselves." The man yelled into the darkness. He hadn't moved. "You're all coming with me, whether you like it or not."

Christopher's eyes began to adjust to the dim light. He could just make out Squeaks near him, also hugging the floor, his lips moving in a silent prayer. He shifted to his knees, preparing to charge the guy when a glint from the gun stopped him.

The Rogue Code

"Don't move, kid." He said. It was the last thing he said as a loud thud sounded. The gun dropped to the warehouse floor and the goon crumpled soon after. Celeste stood, her bat ready for another swing.

"What are we waiting for? Let's MOVE!" she yelled.

Jonas scooped up what belongings he could and they raced out into the evening, gathering their bikes.

"I have informed the authorities of another disturbance." Solomon's voice came from Christopher's wrist, "Do you need other assistance?"

Christopher looked at the bikes, and then Jonas with his arms full. He smiled.

"Solomon, I think we need a lift."

7

Tremain set his teacup down, having just drained the last sip. In front of him sat an empty plate that once held a few tea cakes and sandwich sections. He wiped his mouth and gave a contented sigh. The large open bay windows in the far wall let a nice breeze flow through the room, bringing with it the scent of flowers. Other than the table and a few console tables along the wall, the room was bare.

"Nothing compares to a good sandwich." He said and smiled at his host.

Lyda Stryker smiled at him over the rim of her tea cup, her plate still full, having not been touched.

"It's nice to see you have good appetite,

Tremain." She placed her cup down and gave him a shrewd look, "Tell me, how did you get involved in science?"

Tremain blinked as he pondered the question.

"You know, I've never been asked that before," he pushed around a crumb on his plate, "I guess it all started when I was a boy. My father gave me a telescope for one of my birthdays. I learned about planets, the galaxy and the larger universe, and decided to do something like that when I grew up. I devoted myself to science," he looked up, "I began to create things, thinking I'd make myself famous," he chuckled, "Until I realized the things I made sometimes had a habit of exploding. Spectacularly." He spread his hands out, "But one or two inventions actually did some good. I had a sort of epiphany. What I was a part of was bigger than me or my ego. I could actually help people. I was already an intern at the lab, so it wasn't a huge leap to stay on and use the platform I had to really make things better for people on a larger scale."

Lyda frowned.

"So your drive to create more and more technology came from a place of altruism?"

"If you like," Tremain leaned forward, "and how

did you, with your strong opinions against it, get involved in a tech company?"

Lyda waved the question away.

"A means to an end."

"What sort of end are you talking about?"

Lyda sat back and steepled her fingers, resting her elbows on her thighs.

"Tell me more about your time in college."

Tremain was about to answer when his tablet chirped.

"Forgive me, one moment." He said as Lyda graciously waved him on.

Frowning, he unrolled the tablet from his pocket and read the message. His eyes grew wide.

"What is it?" Lyda demanded.

Tremain cleared his throat.

"It seems you have a snake in your garden." Tremain pointed to the message with his free hand, "The virus that affected the autonomous car system came from this company." He stood, "There's proof."

Lyda stood and came around the table, her hands behind her back.

"May I see?" She placed her left hand on the small of Tremain's back as she came up to him.

Tremain turned the tablet to show her, when he stiffened. Trembling, his tablet dropped to the floor.

His eyes, wide with pain and shock stared accusingly at her.

"S-s-s-s-s-eriously?" he hissed out as he crumpled to the floor.

Lyda removed the taser ring from her hand and replaced it in her pocket. She pushed a button on her wristband and two large men came into the room.

"Take him to my yacht." She walked over and glared out the windows, not seeing the view. Behind her, one of the two men picked up Tremain's tablet, rolled it up and replaced it in the scientist's pocket, then the two lifted his limp body, and carried him out the door they came in from. Lyda frowned.

A member of security entered the room.

"Ma'am. We've found the programmer. One of our men is bringing him in now." He stiffened and held his hand to his ear. His expression blanched.

"What is it?" Lyda demanded.

"H-he got away." The man stammered.

"WHAT?!"

"He had help. Some kids. That's all we know."

Lyda's hands balled into fists.

"FIND HIM! And get those kids too!" She yelled at the man.

He jerked and ran out of the room.

Lyda took deep breaths as she composed herself, her hand firmly clasped around the locket she wore.

Time was running out.

8

Christopher, Celeste, Squeaks, Tenny, Zach, and a cleaned up Jonas stood in the waiting room just outside of Senator Markus' office. The Senator's secretary gave them disapproving glances as she answered call after call. The door to the office opened and Markus beckoned them in, his hair in disarray, the bags under his eyes more prominent than ever.

"Come on in, kids." He murmured as he stepped aside. They filed in. "You said this was urgent?" Markus asked as he plopped in the chair behind his desk. He let out a sigh, then started as he noticed Jonas. "And who's this?"

"Senator," Christopher said as he stepped forward and indicated the programmer, "This is

Jonas. He used to work for Stryker Technologies. We think he may know what's going on." Markus' eyes opened wide and his eyebrows shot up.

"That is indeed good news," he said as he clapped his hands once and rubbed his palms together, "So, what is going on? Why the disruptions? There are laws against these things ..." he looked thoughtful for a moment, "unless you've already shared this with Tremain." Markus turned to Christopher, "Is he getting it all figured out then?" he asked, "Is that why he's not here?"

Christopher nodded.

"Yes, he's at Lyda Stryker's office now."

"Oh, is he?" Markus nodded, frowning. "This is serious. If Stryker Technology is behind all of this ... those apps are on every tablet, every smart system everywhere." He glanced at Jonas, "I should have you questioned for your part in it."

Christopher had a sudden thought.

He scrambled to unroll his tablet, the others looking at him in confusion.

"Solomon!" Christopher called into the tablet.

"Yes, Christopher, how may I be of assistance?"

"The signature we showed you. Can you identify it in other systems?"

"I am already working on it."

The Rogue Code

Jonas tapped Christopher on the shoulder.

"I only put my signature in the one system. I personally didn't break into any others. What I do know is I didn't work on any virus, I wouldn't have done that." He looked at the Senator. "Please, I might be able to get back into the Stryker system and find out what the whole thing looks like. Let me help fix this."

Another call came in for the Senator. He gestured the teenagers to hold on as he answered. On the screen before him, Colonel Griffiths' face appeared.

"Colonel," Markus said, "how can I help you?"

The Colonel's face, normally serious, grew even graver.

"Looks like we have some trouble up here on Platform One, Senator. I can't seem to get in touch with the professor, so I tried you."

Markus cleared his throat. Platform One orbited the planet in a geosynchronous path, serving as a tether for the space elevator. What problems could they be having that the Colonel had to call for help?

"Tremain is tracking down a serious security issue at the moment. What's your trouble?"

Griffiths paused a moment, looked to his left, then his right, and leaned closer to the camera.

"Our systems up here seem to be compromised." As if in response, the screen flickered and split down the center before coming in clear again, "if we don't find the cause, we'll be dead in the water, so to speak." His face seemed to be carved from stone, "if that happens, we won't be able to keep ourselves stable. I don't need to explain further, do I?"

Markus wiped his forehead and shook his head.

"Understood, Colonel. I'll make this a priority."

He disconnected the call and stood up, his gaze on the teenagers, who all looked back at him with pale faces and shocked looks.

"This is getting more s-serious." Squeaks stuttered.

"Christopher, when your uncle returns, I need to speak with him." Markus said, his voice grave.

Christopher nodded.

"We'll do what we can to help, Senator."

Markus glared at Jonas.

"Help them. Fix this. I can make sure that gets taken into account. Keep me posted." He sat down and sighed once more, "Now I need to inform the rest of the Council." He smiled grimly, "wish me luck."

The teenagers and Jonas filed out of the office as Markus put in his call.

. . .

As they exited the Senate building, Tenny asked the obvious question.

"Guys, this just got huge. How are we going to be able to stop this?"

Christopher stopped in front of a park bench.

"I think this is where Jonas comes in. If he can get into the Stryker systems again, we'll have a better idea of the big picture. We can't wait for my uncle. Solomon can help us figure out our steps after that."

"There are two things that Stryker is probably going to do," Jonas said, holding up a finger, "One, which she's already doing, is to cause as much confusion as she can before she does the second thing." He held up another finger and paused.

"Which is?" Tenny interrupted.

Jonas gave him an annoyed look.

"I kept my ears open when I was working there. She's working on something big that I wasn't a part of, but it had to do with using your lab's AI."

"Wait," Christopher grabbed Jonas' arm, "She's after Solomon?"

"That's the AI?" Jonas' wild grin made him look much younger. "That's so cool."

Christopher's tension was palpable.

"We need to get back to the lab as fast as possible."

"G good idea." Squeaks said as he pushed his glasses up on his nose again. His nervous nature beginning to show.

Celeste grabbed Christopher's arm.

"I feel like dead weight here. I don't know how I can help."

Christopher knit his brows together.

"We'll figure it out. Make it up as we go along."

Celeste smiled.

"Will I still need my baseball bat?"

Zach giggled.

Tenny leaned towards Christopher and mock-whispered in his ear.

"Remind me not to ever get on her bad side."

Markus disconnected his call and rubbed his face. That had not gone well. At all. The other senators, while agreeing that the issues with Platform One were serious, they felt the entire situation would be solved soon by Tremain and had decided to sit and wait and see what happens. Short-sighted lazy good-for-nothings. Not for the first time Markus wondered why he ever went into politics. He sat and brooded for a moment.

What would Tremain do?

If a virus, or whatever, was attacking their most vulnerable systems, and their security was unable to arrest its progress, then the logical solution would be to fight fire with fire, or virus with virus.

The realization came like a slap to the face.

It was so obvious.

Why hadn't he thought of it sooner?

He looked up to the ceiling.

"Solomon?"

"I am here, Senator." Came the reply.

"Begin Operation Cloud."

"I shall begin immediately."

Markus sat back and drummed his fingers on his desk.

DEEP UNDERGROUND, in multiple locations, racks of computers hummed to life. As each component lit up, the hum grew louder, and a series of clicks, whirs and other noises filled the spaces. Each location, identical in layout, could only be accessed by a security door with a locking system created by Tremain. Only he and Markus knew how to enter the node.

Along one wall of hardware, a film of glass sat mounted to the rack. Below that sat a mechanical keyboard. The film of glass flared to life. A green cursor flashed on the screen, rapidly replaced by the words:

This is Solomon.

9

Tremain came to awareness slowly. He wanted to move, but stopped himself.

What had happened? One moment he was drinking tea, then ... *ZAP!*

His eyes snapped open.

Lyda.

Not moving, his eyes roamed the room he found himself in. He was alone and lay on his side in a bed.

A quite plush and comfortable bed.

In other circumstances, he might enjoy this.

Through a small window in the wall he faced he could see palm fronds waving in the breeze.

Not near the lab then.

He groaned as he rolled to his back, feeling the stiffness where Lyda had tasered him. His shoulder felt stiff too. He felt around and winced as he hit a tender spot. He'd been injected with something too, he was certain.

Obviously, she was the culprit behind the disturbances.

He chided himself on walking right into the spider's den, so to speak.

He hadn't known.

How could he?

That didn't help explain why she had kidnapped him.

Nor did it help him to figure out what her end goal might be.

He sat up and examined the room.

The far wall beyond the foot of the bed contained a door and a floor-to-ceiling bookcase. Tremain stood, shuffled over, and tried the doorhandle. It opened smoothly to show a large bathroom with enclosed shower and separate bathtub. He gave an appraising nod to the aesthetics. Fine tile lined the walls and shower stall, modeled after a classic European motif. Very nice.

He turned on the cold tap and splashed some water in his face, helping to shrug off the effects of whatever drug he'd been injected with.

Frowning, he turned his attention to the book-

The Rogue Code

case. Each shelf was full of books with subjects ranging from fiction to astrophysics. Whatever else she was, Lyda Stryker was a well-read person. Assuming, of course, she had read all these books. He ran his fingers down a shelf, noticing the lack of dust.

A cleaning staff, perhaps? He had a hard time envisioning Lyda with a duster in hand.

He shook his head, trying to clear out the remaining cobwebs. Stay on task, he reminded himself.

A wardrobe stood silent on the wall with another door. The way out perhaps?

Tremain felt the rolled up tablet shift in his pocket. He didn't need a door to escape, now did he? Reaching into his pocket, he unfurled the tablet. Finger poised over the icon for his transmitter, he paused. It glowed at him, beckoning, inviting him to come home.

He snapped the tablet shut and replaced it in his pocket.

Not until he had some answers.

He walked over to the window and looked out.

He could see the grounds stretch out before him to a cliff edge, with the churning sea beyond that. Palm trees dotted the landscape. A golf-cart with three men, all dressed in crisp white uniforms, headed away somewhere on a well-trimmed and paved pathway.

"Suddenly I feel as if I'm in a spy movie." Tremain said to himself.

The door chimed. He turned as he heard the lock disengage and the door opened to reveal a small woman in yet another crisp white uniform. She looked at him with a bland expression on her face, as if she didn't care what she saw, she just did her job.

"Come along now," she said, "your tour is about to start."

"What tour?" Tremain barked, his irritation clear, "I'd prefer some answers!"

The woman smiled and gestured out the door. He wasn't going to get anything out of her. Seeing as he didn't have much of a choice, he followed her out of the room.

A short corridor lead them to a landing of sorts which looked out over a gorgeous sunken sitting room. Bookcases lined every section of wall that didn't have a window, their shelves either full of books or displaying knickknacks or other objects that could have been antiques. Dark moldings were visible along the floor as well as along the ceiling. A large, rustic fireplace nestled between bookcases, the blaze within filling the room with a cozy warmth. Tremain noticed the view out every window captured the coast and rolling ocean.

Breathtaking.

"Ah, you're awake." Lyda's voice came from below him. Tremain looked down to see her lounging on a plush leather couch, "I wondered how long you'd be out. I guessed at the dosage."

Tremain's thin smile showed little humor.

"You have an odd way of inviting one to your ... do I call this a compound?"

Lyda stretched and smiled back at him.

"It's my own little kingdom, Tremain. I have this entire island to myself," she gestured to the couch opposite her, "come, sit, and let's talk."

Tremain took the few stairs into the sunken living room. He gave a glance around as he sat down.

"You do have excellent taste, I'll give you that," his sharp gaze turned to her, "for a kidnapper."

Lyda laughed and waved that off.

"When I'm done, Tremain, kidnapping will be the least of your worries," she leaned forward, "I'm about to change the world for the better."

Tremain's heart beat faster as alarm gripped him.

"So the virus in the auto system ..."

She paused a moment, her brows knit in confusion. Then her eyes widened.

"Oh! You thought that was a virus?" she giggled a little in surprise. "You really have no idea?"

Tremain regarded her with the coldest stare he could muster.

"What are you planning to do?" he asked, his voice almost a growl.

"Like I said in my presentation ... was that only a couple of nights ago?" she shook her head, "time passes by so quick these days. I said technology was evil and should be stopped."

Tremain stood and began to pace the room from bookcase to over-large fireplace.

"All technology?"

"Whatever drives us apart."

Tremain stopped pacing and faced her, his fists balled at his sides.

"Assuming you can, how do you propose eradicating all technology?"

Lyda smiled, shifted in her seat, bringing her legs up underneath her, as if she were lounging by the pool.

"Before we get into those details, let me ask you, did you know it was me before you came to ... apologize?"

Tremain blinked, surprised by the question.

"To be honest, no. I didn't realize it was you specifically who masterminded all of it until you tased me during our tea."

"Excellent." Lyda clapped theatrically.

Tremain placed his hands on the back of the couch and leaned over.

"Now, tell me how you plan on destroying the world as we know it."

10

Christopher sat at his uncle's desk in the lab, Squeaks, Tenny, Celeste, and Zach gathered around him on folding chairs. Jonas stood apart from the group, chewing on a thumbnail. They all wore a look of shock.

"That news is bad. Real bad." Squeaks said to nobody in particular.

They had entered the lab to catch the end of a news program Desmond had on in the background. It had showed empty motorways due to a lack of confidence in the autonomous systems after the latest failure. People had chosen to not leave their homes out of fear, despite the government's assurances. As a result, almost all business had ground to a halt. Senators were being inundated with calls and complaints.

"It'll be worse if we can't figure this thing out." Christopher said, "What we need to do is isolate the virus."

"I believe I have discovered the cause." Solomon's voice came through the speakers, "It is not a virus, as we believed, but something else I have yet to determine. I am investigating, but b-b-b-b-b-b-but I will need t-t-t-t-t-t-to . . ." The voice dissolved into static.

"Solomon!" Christopher yelled.

Desmond hustled over to them.

"What's going on with him?" he asked.

"I don't know, he stuttered, then stopped talking."

"I am ... operational." Solomon's voice boomed out, "I am currently under assault by numerous intrusion attempts. T-t-t-t-t-they're increasing exponentially every minute. My protective firewalls are keeping them at bay for the moment, however, this is taking resources away from more important tasks."

Jonas looked impressed.

"So, it's started."

Christopher's glare stopped Jonas. He turned his attention back to Solomon.

"How do you know it's not a virus? What can we do to help?"

"There is no sign of malware in any system I have checked. I have, however, found evidence of another presence. I have yet to determine what it is. To your second question, I have implemented a contingency plan created by Tremain and Senator Markus."

Zach looked confused. Celeste, standing next to him, had the same look on her face.

"What does that even mean? Another presence?" she asked.

Christopher, breathing hard, turned to her.

"I don't know yet. But my uncle and I talked about a backup plan for Solomon. I didn't know he'd gone ahead and done it." He said.

"Done what?" She asked, bringing up her hands in exasperation.

"He called it Operation Cloud. It's a series of networked nodes, huge computer systems, all in hidden locations. In case of any problems with Solomon's systems here, he could transfer himself to any one, or all of them. Either that, or they'd already have Solomon's source code installed, and it just has to boot up and sync up. I don't know, we didn't talk about it much after that."

"Well said, Christopher." Solomon's voice sounded distorted, "please stand by."

"What do we do now?" Tenny asked, looking bored, but his arms folded across his chest betrayed his tension.

"I guess we wait while Jonas digs into the Stryker systems."

Static sounded through the speakers, then silence.

"Wow." Squeaks murmured, "Can he network himself quickly?"

Christopher shook his head while shrugging.

Jonas wrung his hands.

"Not to get too ahead of myself, but I need a terminal. If I can get myself into the Stryker systems, and I can figure out what she's got planned, your AI can follow past my hacking, infiltrate it, and stop everything where it starts."

"Won't that be just like handing Solomon over to her?" Christopher asked.

"Not at all! They won't be able to do a thing with him once he's there. It'll be like we're the virus in their system."

Christopher thought about it for a moment before making his decision.

"I'll take any advantage we can have. Do it."

"How much time do we have?" Zach asked.

Christopher shrugged again.

"I don't know. I'm just assuming we don't have a lot of time here." He glanced up at the digital clock on the wall, then looked around the lab, "And where the heck is my uncle?"

TREMAIN LEANED over the couch back, eyes firmly locked with Lyda Stryker's.

"Tell me how."

Lyda stood, unfolding herself as if she didn't have a care in the world. She was in control of the situation and she knew it.

"Why bore you with the minutiae, Tremain? In a few hours it'll all be over, and there's not a single thing you can do to stop me. Now," she gestured around, "Would you like a tour? I'd love to show you my home."

"A tour?" Tremain spluttered, "I'd rather have a root canal!"

Lyda seemed to glide around the couch until she was standing in front of Tremain, who turned to face her. She casually reached up and straightened a lapel of his lab coat.

"Let's not be rude. I would be a very bad host if I

didn't give an honored guest a tour of my island, now would I?"

Tremain swallowed. The menace emanating off her was almost palpable.

"That would indeed be rude, wouldn't it?" he grimaced, "a tour would be ... lovely."

Lyda smiled and patted his cheek.

"There you go," She purred, and led him away, pulling at his lab coat, "now where shall we start?"

"You're the tour guide, not I."

She released his coat and clasped her hands in front of her chest.

"I have just the place to begin."

Tremain followed her, a grim look on his face, drumming a pattern with his fingers on his pocket.

IN THE LAB, the doors blew open as the Senator burst in. Breathless, he walked over to where Christopher sat, placed his hands on the desk and composed himself.

"I ran all the way," Markus huffed and puffed, "had to escape the phone calls." He looked up, his eyes full of seriousness, "I need to resolve this crisis fast." He glanced around, "Where's Tremain?"

"Good question," Celeste answered him, "he's not back yet."

"Not back?" Markus frowned, making his mustache stick out comically. Celeste stifled a snicker.

"I haven't tracked his tablet, though," Christopher chimed in, "I didn't think it was necessary, but now seeing as he's been gone so long …" He opened the tracking program and ran it for his uncle's tablet. "It shows him … in the ocean?"

"He went swimming?" Squeaks piped up, "Man, and here we are doing all the work!"

Tenny jabbed Squeaks, causing his glasses to slip.

"Shut it, Squeaks. You know Tremain doesn't swim."

Christopher listened to his friends with half an ear. Something didn't add up. His uncle wouldn't have just left to go swimming … especially not when there was any sort of crisis. Where exactly was he? He zoomed in on the map. It still showed ocean. He zoomed in further.

There.

A small dot of land appeared as he zoomed in yet further. The legend on the map designated it as a private island.

"He's on a private island." Christopher called out.

Markus sighed with relief.

"Well, as long as he's safe ... wait ... an island?" he looked up to the ceiling, "Solomon, can you tell me who owns this island?"

He was greeted with silence.

"Um ... Senator ... Solomon is networking himself to keep a bunch of steps ahead of the hackers trying to get to him." Christopher explained, "Operation Cloud. He might be out of communication for a while."

Markus nodded.

"Oh, that's right. I did activate those node-things Tremain had set up months ago. I don't know if he'd finished testing them yet, but I'm glad I made that call."

"That's Lyda Stryker's island." Jonas piped up from his terminal, having glanced at Christopher's screen, his hands flying over the keyboard as he talked.

"Why didn't you speak up sooner?" Markus asked, looking at the hacker warily.

"Kinda busy here too." Jonas' eyes never left his screen.

Christopher leaned into the senator.

"He's trying to get us into the Stryker systems so we can get Solomon to shut it down from the inside."

Markus' eyes widened at that and he nodded. He gestured to the programmer.

"Um ... hack faster."

11

The lab speakers burst to life.

"I have located Tremain." Solomon said.

"So have we, genius," Tenny whispered to Squeaks, who shushed him.

"He's on an island, Solomon," Christopher stated.

"He is sending a message. It is fortunate that I detected it."

Christopher stood up. A message?

"What kind of message? Why wouldn't he just call in?"

"If not just, you know, come back to the lab ..." Zach muttered to Tenny's amusement.

"It is a passive signal. Would you like to hear Tremain's message? He sent it in Morse code."

Markus frowned.

"Morse code? We used that as boys to send messages in class." He tilted his head at Tenny, "infuriated the teachers, let me tell you, but you know, boys will be boys."

Tenny smiled, leaned back and crossed his arms.

"I get you, Senator." He said through his smile.

Markus narrowed his eyes at Tenny and was about to say something when Christopher stood up.

"AHEM! The message, Solomon?"

"To paraphrase, Tremain states that unless we stop it in the next few hours, all technology will cease functioning due to Lyda Stryker. He has yet to ascertain how she will achieve this."

Silence fell in the lab. Even Desmond stopped to listen.

"That's not a lot of time." Squeaks muttered.

"Thanks captain obvious." Tenny retorted.

"Guys, cut it out!" Christopher yelled. All eyes turned to him. "We can't just give up. Solomon, we think the something else is you? All the intrusion attempts on you, can we stop them?"

"I'm almost in." Jonas shouted from his terminal.

"Solomon," Christopher said, "We're trying to

break into the Stryker systems. I hope that gives you some advantage to get them before they get you."

"I will do my best."

A burst of static came from the speakers.

Celeste scratched her ear.

"So, Tremain is on an island owned by the woman he was going to apologize to," She started, "that must have been one heck of an apology."

Christopher threw her a look.

"That's not the way my uncle works," he said, "He would have a very good reason to be there."

Celeste raised her eyebrows, smiling.

"Not that!" Cristopher objected.

"We're wasting time." Markus broke in.

"I'm in!" Jonas yelled. His fingers flew across the virtual keyboard as he typed. Squeaks and Zach rushed to Jonas' chair.

Jonas' raised his hands as Solomon took control. Christopher watched him, hoping he was right in trusting the hacker.

Tenny growled from his seat.

"What the heck is that?" he asked.

Jonas leaned his head back.

"Guys!" he yelled, "I think the Stryker apps are being used as a conduit for ..." he trailed off.

"Oh no." Tenny whispered.

"Shit's getting real." Squeaks whispered back.

"We have to delete the apps!" Tenny shouted.

Zach, sitting and waiting, threw his hands up.

"Seriously? And here I was almost beating my best score!"

Senator Markus went over to Tenny's terminal. His eyes widened as Tenny pointed out what he'd found.

"Delete them! All of them!" Markus almost shouted.

The teenagers each pulled out their devices and deleted every Stryker app they had. Zach took the most time as he had the most apps.

"And there goes my streak of finding the signature first." He muttered.

"Look on the bright side," Squeaks called back to Zach, "At least you found the most important one!"

Zach brightened.

"Yeah, good point!"

Christopher walked over to Jonas and looked at the screen. His eyes widened.

"This is not good." Jonas whispered.

How much time did they really have?

12

Tremain looked over the steaming lagoon below him as Lyda Stryker gestured to it, a proud look on her face. Despite himself, he found the island impressive.

Lyda had given him the grand tour, driving around in a golf cart. Most of her compound had been built underground. On the surface were farms and ranches, recreational areas, beaches, etc. The island could sustain itself indefinitely. Now Tremain glared out over the underground lagoon, a single pier jutting into the water. Two large boats and a smaller craft were moored to it, bobbing with the motion of the water. Far to his left, he could see a large group of large tubes and conduits snaking from the water into the rock face. He felt sticky in the thick, humid air.

"This island sits on a thermal vent," she was saying, "I use the emissions to help power this island." She pointed to the pipes, "Deep beneath the island I have a set of turbines that use the force from the vents to generate electricity. And of course, a pleasant side effect is I have an unending source of hot water."

"And the rest of your power comes from solar energy?"

"Exactly." Lyda crossed her arms and tilted her chin up at Tremain, "You're not impressed."

Tremain sniffed and wiped an invisible speck of dirt from his lab coat.

"On the contrary, I'm quite amazed at it all, but I'm wondering how someone with such disdain for technology has used the very same hated thing in powering her island," he turned toward her, "in fact, you are such a contradiction it's mind-boggling."

"Go on." She prodded.

"You're the head of a prominent software company, you have your own private island where you grow your own food, raise your own livestock, all with modern methods. You've shown me your solar collectors and now this thermal vent power plant," he waved his hands in frustration, "yet here you are ready to bring all of this to an end. You'll be hurting yourself as well."

Lyda smiled at the scientist.

"I'm willing to make the sacrifice. Besides, all this is self-sustaining. No outside technology is used. No matter what, this island is protected."

"So, you will be the only one who gets to live in comfort." Tremain shook his head as he shoved his hands into his lab coat pockets, "I can't help but think of all the people on life support, those with pacemakers, or artificial hearts and limbs. What will happen to them? What about food storage? When winter comes, thousands will die."

"Sacrifices must be made, Tremain. If we are to survive, those who are too dependent on technology will ..."

"Die." Tremain finished for her.

Lyda pursed her lips and gestured for Tremain to follow.

"Come along, Tremain, there's more for you to see."

They climbed a flight of stairs, at the top of which was a solid wall. Lyda touched one section. With a beep, the wall slid aside to reveal a control room.

Lyda led Tremain into the room, and up another flight of stairs to a catwalk that ran along the entire interior. The catwalk was also lined with computer terminals, some manned, others empty.

The wall where they stood was dominated by a map of the continents, with dotted lines indicating the paths of satellites as they orbited the globe.

The circular room below them had high walls with windows at the very top, letting in natural light. A circular bank of computer terminals sat in the center of the room, each one manned by a programmer in various states of casual wear.

"Couldn't get the programmers to wear the uniforms?" Tremain asked, after glancing around the room.

Lyda waved him off, as she turned to gaze in pride over her employees.

"These are my prized programmers. The ones who showed the most promise, the most creativity, and had the fewest scruples. They are merely doing a job. They will be well compensated for their efforts."

"How well did you treat the one who left his calling card?"

"Does it matter? We'll find him, but soon, it'll be a talent that will no longer be necessary," She gestured to the ceiling, where a large holo-screen showed a count-down. Ninety minutes left before the end, sending the planet into chaos. "Tick-tock goes the clock."

"You said this wasn't a virus, but something else. That makes sense, as a virus wouldn't eliminate all technology, only incapacitate it for a while." Tremain's eyes narrowed as he confronted Lyda, "What did you do?"

Lyda's grin grew wider.

"Fight fire with fire, I always say. You think you're the smartest man on the planet, don't you? Your own hubris will be the end of you." She stepped closer, her eyes alight with excitement ... or madness. "Your own creation will destroy it all."

Tremain stood stunned. He shook his head.

"Solomon? His firewalls are impenetrable. Not only did I create the originals, but he's built in more security himself."

Tremain crossed his arms and rubbed his chin in frustration. His shoulders hunched with the tension he felt coursing through him. They couldn't break through Solomon's protections, could they? Another thought occurred to him.

Fight fire with fire?

Fight fire with ...

Oh no.

"You've created another AI!" he shouted.

Lyda clapped theatrically.

"Finally the genius figures it out."

"How did you … ?"

Lyda grinned widely.

"You're not the only one who has the resources, Tremain. You once published a paper about the benefits of AI. Do you remember?"

"Yes, but I don't see … "

"And what did you say about how one could go about creating said AI?"

Tremain thought a moment, his head cocked as he tried to figure out where she was going with this. Then it hit him.

"You used a brain scan?!" he said, his shock written on his face.

"I did. A great short cut, eliminating months of writing code."

Tremain took a deep breath, calming himself.

"The problem with brain scans is they are unreliable, and eventually quite unstable. That was also in the paper I wrote."

Lyda waved her hand dismissively.

"When you have the best programmers money can buy, you can do anything, Tremain."

"Whose brain scan did you use?"

Lyda smiled once more.

Tremain closed his eyes and took another deep breath.

"You used your own scan, didn't you?"

Lyda wore a look of triumph on her face.

"Who better to help me than myself? At the very least, it's someone I know I can trust."

"So the disruptions were caused by this AI?"

"Exactly. She disguised herself as a virus, but the end result is the same. Confusion and chaos before she helps me take control of your AI."

"You've told me how, Lyda," he said after a long pause, "now I need to know the why. Why are you doing this?"

Lyda gestured for him to follow. She led him back into the living room he was originally brought to. She waved away any staff that were in the room. In moments, they were alone, she on the same couch as before, Tremain sitting ram-rod straight opposite her. The air felt thick with tension.

"I have watched our society change over the years. With each new step forward, it seems as if we lose another piece of our humanity. It's like our entire society is on life support. We can only watch it wither and die." She let that hang in the air a moment. "Have you ever lost someone close to you?" As she asked, she fondled the locket around her neck. Tremain had noticed it before, but hadn't given it much thought. He blinked, confused by the change of topics.

"Like everyone else, I've lost family members. Why do you ask?"

"You want to know the causes of my crusade, don't you?" She glared at him as she stood and took the locket from her neck. She opened it, ran a finger across the portraits inside, then glared at Tremain again. The hatred in her eyes hit him like a wall. She shoved the locket towards him, the chain hanging loose below her hand, "Here are two of my reasons. I lost a most beloved sister and her daughter to technology. Technology YOU invented, Tremain. She was a contemporary of yours, I believe. Perhaps you remember her? Her name was Aziza."

13

Tremain couldn't have been more shocked if Aziza herself had walked into the room.

Did he remember her?

With his near-perfect memory, he could never forget her.

He didn't even have to look at the locket thrust out at him to recall her face, the huge almond shaped eyes, the luxurious hair that draped over her shoulders. He could also never forget the flawed transmitter beam engulfing her and her daughter, Leesa. How her countenance had changed from one of triumph to one of fear as she dissolved, torn apart by the energies she had no idea she had unleashed.

Leesa, at her mother's command, had infiltrated Tremain's lab, had become an intern, and had subsequently stolen some old, scrapped plans which included the initial drawings for Tremain's matter transmitter. With that in hand, they had built their own version.

That had been their fatal mistake.

The faulty transmitter had been their only escape after finding what Aziza had surmised to be an ancient weapon but had turned out to be nothing more than a complex irrigation system. Before the authorities could arrest them, Leesa had activated the transmitter.

They had never tested it on an organic subject.

Tremain's attention snapped back to the present to see Lyda replacing the locket around her neck.

Aziza's sister.

He hadn't known Aziza had a sister.

"So you blame me?" Tremain asked, his voice low.

"Who else is to blame? You invented the technology that killed her. You are responsible. As punishment, I am stopping technology from running rampant across the planet. Stopping the very thing you hold so dear." She sat back down onto the couch, the contempt in her face a palpable thing.

Tremain's anger erupted.

"You can start by putting much of that responsibility firmly on Aziza's shoulders!" He yelled, "Those plans were faulty and were marked as such. Had she paid attention, she would have realized there was a reason they were being scrapped. You can't blame me for your own sister's lack of focus!"

"Your precious technology killed her!" Lyda shouted, then took a deep breath and calmed herself. She sat back, relaxing her back and shoulders, "I have lived with this for too long, Tremain."

"How long have you been plotting this ... retribution?" he finally asked.

Lyda lounged for a moment before crossing her arms and glaring at him once more.

"After her death, her foundation fell to me, her only living relative. I transformed it, folding it into my own company, building my influence over time, expanding my reach."

"So that's what happened. After the initial investigation, the Tyndall Foundation fell off the map. You absorbed it."

"I had become disillusioned with this entire industry long before. Each time a new app released,

I saw more and more people downloading it. I was becoming rich off the idleness of others. Our society will rot while we all play games. I refuse to let that happen. I will make sure no-one else dies from technology gone wild."

"What is that?" Squeaks asked, a tremor in his voice.

Jonas took a deep breath and scratched his head.

"That, is a very complex, automatic system. If I'm seeing it correctly, I think it's another AI."

"You are not wrong, Jonas." Solomon replied. His voice sounded distant, "I have avoided detection for the moment, but I believe this entity is the cause of our recent troubles."

"How are you going to proceed?" Christopher asked.

"I will attempt to shadow the AI to see if I can ascertain its goals. If I may make a suggestion, I believe it is using the Stryker app network to insert itself into various systems. Deleting those apps may slow it down."

"We've already begun," Markus said, startling Tenny, "I've also spread the word out to all the Senators. Let's see if I can finally light a fire under their rears. It's time to stop being spectators. They have to act now, or else."

Desmond came over and sat down.

"I don't know about you all, but I'm getting too old for this stress."

Tremain paced the living room, acutely aware of the seconds ticking by.

Precious seconds.

"You do realize you will be doing more harm than good?" he talked fast, the words streaming out of his mouth, "With everything electronic gone, there will be no light, there will be no heat. Without freezers or refrigeration, food will spoil. People will starve. The loss of life in the hospitals alone will be horrendous! Once the vaccines run out, all sorts of extinct illnesses will make a comeback. Measles, polio, smallpox … all of it will come back. Lives are at stake! In our little talk the other night, you do remember how I said that Pandora's Box was open? What makes you think technology won't make a comeback?"

Lyda glanced at her wrist band and smiled.

"Our dependence on all technology has made our society weak. We rely on these devices to do all our work for us." She stood and walked over to the fireplace, which had been lit by the staff. She grabbed a poker and began shoving it into the logs, "By eliminating it all, I'll force us to return to our roots. To come together as a people to help each other, to grow as a society like our ancestors did."

"You'll be sending us back to the stone age!"

"Maybe, but for a short time only. Remember, you can do nothing to stop me."

Tremain stopped pacing and nodded.

"You're right, of course. I can't. Not from here." He reached into his pocket and yanked out his tablet. He was just about to press the transmitter icon when the tip of the poker pierced the screen from behind. It shorted out and went blank.

"Not. So. Fast." Lyda said, yanking the poker back, taking the now ruined tablet with it. She shoved it into the fire, where the flames engulfed it. The plastic began to melt, oozing into the burning embers.

"Thank goodness for backups," Tremain muttered, then he glared at Lyda, "apparently I'm at your mercy."

Her cold smile chilled him.

"To answer your unspoken question, when the time is right, I will say what technology is allowed to return. My AI will see that my orders are followed to the letter."

"And who made you emperor? Is this what Aziza would have wanted?"

Lyda barked out a humorless laugh. She brandished the poker like a sword. Tremain backed up a step or two, hands out in front of him.

"What do you know of my sister? What she would have wanted or not?"

"I know she craved power. Oh she'd be all over what you're doing now, but all this death and destruction? How does this honor her memory?"

Lyda threw the poker back into its holder, her frown deepening.

"My sister's legacy will be the end of rampant technology. I will retain tight control over it all. At least one member of our family will have the respect and power she so craved."

Tremain gestured around the living room.

"Seems to me you already have that with your software empire. How does condemning thousands to death help?"

Lyda walked over to Tremain, bringing her right hand hard across his face. He blinked back the pain and glowered at her.

"Do not moralize with me." She stalked off.

Tremain rubbed his cheek. She did have a good right hook, he'd give her that. His mind raced, trying to think of ways to stop the coming apocalypse.

Feeling his frustration mount, he ran to catch up with Lyda.

14

Lyda fumed.

How dare he question her.

She re-entered her control room, feeling pride as she surveyed her kingdom. Tremain didn't understand. He couldn't understand.

Her family had lived in a remote part of the continent, her father away most of the time doing research. What kind of research, she never bothered to find out. She accepted her father's absences as a fact of life. Her mother kept house.

Lyda had spent years being home-schooled and reading everything she could get her hands on. Learning to read at an early age, she became voracious. She read poetry, literature, anything. She learned all about mankind's history. As she grew, those books became her life-line to another life, another kind of world.

As a nine-year-old, she kept looking at the map, trying to find London, New York, the path of the Mississippi River ... all the things she'd read about. Her mother laughed at her innocence.

"No, Lyda, you're looking at the wrong map." She said, "You won't find those places there. We don't live on that world any more. We're on New Earth, not the old one."

Lyda's world-view exploded.

She read everything she could about the colonists, about the journey to New Earth, about forging a new life here on a new planet. At first she was overjoyed, but then she became annoyed. Angry.

How dare they?

How could they leave the world that had such wonders? She had been too young to understand about politics, about the turmoil that had prompted some to look beyond the stars for a new home, to make a new start. She could only see what they had left behind.

Aziza was born when Lyda was ten.

The girls helped their mother tend to the garden, where they grew most of their food, and tend to the animals. They had few neighbors and fewer friends.

Aziza's interests were very different from her older sister's. Where Lyda was more cerebral, Aziza's temperament grew to be one of impatience. She hated to wait for anything. She didn't want to learn something new, she wanted to know it now, if not sooner.

Being the younger sister didn't help her either. Second fiddle, she would call it. Her competitive streak became her hallmark.

As the girls grew up, Lyda realized that there was more to living than growing vegetables. There was an entire world out there waiting to be seen.

She took the entrance exams for the University early, getting a perfect score on her first try. Once at college, another new world engulfed her. She finally found out what research her father did. He was a scientist that sometimes performed experiments up on Platform One, which explained his long absences. At first she was proud of the work her father did, but soon grew bitter. All the hardship she grew up with could have been made easier with some of the things her father had around him daily.

At college she made many friends and found she excelled at business. A while later, she and some of her friends started their own company, providing software to the masses.

That was the start of Stryker Technologies.

Aziza eventually joined her sister at University, her time alone tempering her impatience. She quickly became a star in the scientific fields, and gained the interest of a particular upperclassman by the name of Tremain. Lyda watched as her sister's need to be in control of everything became her undoing. She had tried to prevent her sister from stealing Tremain's notes, but failed. After Aziza's prompt dismissal from school, Lyda brought her into the fold at the software company.

With both sisters propelling it forward, the company grew.

Lyda noticed trends. Noticed when societal issues arose and how it corresponded to an increase in app activity. People started tuning real life out and instead immersed themselves in make-believe. She began re-analyzing Earth history, seeing how as technology progressed, it only made some matters worse for the population.

She grew restless.

Aziza's lust for power and control returned full-force. She and Lyda were soon at odds in the company. After a bitter argument, Aziza left. Lyda read soon after that she had married an entrepreneur. She lost touch after that, until she read about her sister's death.

She mourned, even as she found out all she could about the circumstances. She learned the transmitter had been designed by Tremain.

Tremain. Again.

Her anger grew.

She absorbed Aziza's estate into her own, knowing she could use it to create the change she knew the world needed.

She and her sister had grown up in a world without technology.

Technology had killed her sister.

Technology was the problem.

She focused her energy on creating a new vision for herself.

She was going to change the world as well as take her revenge on the one person most responsible for her sister's death.

And here she was on the cusp of doing just that.

Ridding the world of the technology that poisoned it.

She smiled as she folded her arms in front of her.

Out of the corner of her eye, she watched Tremain as he climbed the steps to the catwalk overlooking the hackers. He stood powerless to stop her.

Her smile grew.

THE TEENAGERS in the lab worked furiously, locating and deleting Stryker apps from every system they could, not stopping to even rub the fatigue out of their fingers. Christopher took another glance at the clock.

Time was slipping by. He didn't know how much time they had, but at the rate they were going, they weren't going to make it.

Next to him, Celeste sat staring at nothing.

"People are going to die, aren't they?" she whispered.

"Maybe." Christopher muttered.

Static burst from the speakers. Solomon's voice came through, but muted, as if he were talking to them through a paper tube.

"The AI is breaking through my firewalls, Christopher. I am forced to take that system offline to protect the main lab from infiltration."

"What?" Squeaks and Tenny protested. Zach stayed focused and kept working.

The moments passed, seemed to stretch out to eternity. Christopher found himself staring at a speaker in the wall, hoping Solomon was ok.

"I am now separated from the rest of the lab and the AI are breaking in. It will find nothing of value as I have removed myself from that server. I have fully activated all nodes across the colony. My processing power has increased dramatically. It is a ... heady feeling."

"We're not going to get all the apps erased before the deadline." Christopher said.

"It is of no consequence. I believe I know what the endgame is."

"What does he mean?" Celeste asked.

Christopher shrugged his shoulders at her.

"Endgame?" he asked out loud.

"I can assume the hacking attempt on my system is the event that Tremain spoke about. Since there is no other logical means to destroy all technology."

"Wait ... destroy all technology?" Celeste asked.

"Correct. If the hacking attempts were successful, they would be able to use me to destroy it from the inside, if you will."

"Oh my lords." Celeste whispered.

"They will assume they have achieved their goal. They do not realize I am one step ahead of them."

"So what do we do?" Christopher asked.

Tenny, Squeaks and Zach had stopped working and were now watching Christopher.

"We turn the tables on them, Christopher." Solomon said.

15

In the control room, Tremain watched as the timer inched closer and closer to zero.

He clenched his jaw and twisted his hands around the catwalk railing.

He couldn't stop thinking of Aziza, his one-time flame turned adversary. She wouldn't have wanted this to happen. She wouldn't have condoned the murder of innocent people, all to prove a point.

She did activate the irrigation system, though, not realizing what it actually was, thinking she was using a weapon. Had it been one, she potentially could have killed them all, herself included.

Maybe insanity did run in her family.

Tremain thought again of Solomon, a pawn in this sick game. What was happening to him as Lyda's

AI broke down his defenses? Could it? His mind turned to Christopher, to Celeste ... all the people whose lives would forever be changed.

He had to stop this madness, but how?

Glancing around, he realized he stood alone on the catwalk. Lyda was below, supervising the proceedings, ignoring him.

Nobody was paying any attention.

He inched his way down the catwalk to the stairs, taking them slowly so as not to draw any attention to himself. Once down on the floor, he paused to see if anyone noticed.

Nobody turned to look his way.

Feeling the fluttering of hope blossoming in his chest, he walked out of the control room into the corridor beyond.

He would stop this.

He was going to escape.

He walked quickly, blessing his near-perfect memory as he wound his way through the corridors until he came to a double door.

The lagoon.

He could take the smaller boat, get back to the mainland and find a way to counter the AI, to stop the destruction. Lyda's crusade would cause confusion and hassle, but it could be overcome. If he could not stop her, she would potentially fry every electronic system, from a pocket-watch on up. The world would come to a complete stop. That was something he could not allow.

With this in mind, he opened the doors. The lagoon was unoccupied.

The boats still bobbed against their moorings. Tremain made his way to the smaller of the boats, climbed in and cast off the lines.

He felt a thrill of victory as he sat in the pilot seat and saw the keys were in the ignition. Taking a deep breath and offering up a prayer, he turned the key.

Nothing happened.

No click, no whirr, no … anything. Just nothing.

That wasn't right.

Feeling his chance slip away from him, Tremain turned the key to off and back again.

Still nothing.

He looked to the battery indicator. Full charge. So why wasn't the blasted thing starting?

IN THE CONTROL ROOM, Lyda stood, arms still folded as she surveyed the hackers at work. She glanced up to the catwalk to see it empty.

She frowned.

Where had Tremain gone?

A flashing light on a panel caught her attention.

The lagoon?

She smiled, narrowed her eyes and stalked out of the control room.

Tremain moved from the battery, wiping sweat from his forehead and checking all the connections, back to the pilot's seat, preparing to hotwire the thing, his clothes sticking to him in the heavy, humid air. The double doors opened once more and Lyda strode in.

She held a gun in her hand.

The boat had drifted past the end of the dock as Tremain pulled up an oar. Lyda stalked down the pier.

"Row yourself back over here, Tremain."

"You'll have to shoot me." He replied, dipping the oar into the water.

"And ruin all my fun watching you as your empire falls? I think not." She gestured to the boat with her gun. "What's the matter? Couldn't get it started?"

"Apparently." Tremain grunted as he rowed.

"I suppose I neglected to tell you everything here

is activated bio-metrically. The boats ... and the guns." She aimed and pulled the trigger.

Tremain's oar was ripped out of his hands as the beam hit it, shattering it into fragments.

Huffing, he reached down for the second oar.

"Don't make this any harder on yourself, Tremain," Lyda taunted, "You can't stop what's going to happen. Oh, and don't try to jump and swim either."

Tremain paused and looked over at her.

"And why not? I'm a pretty strong swimmer."

Lyda's smile was thin and without humor.

"Thermal vents, remember? They've heated this water almost to the boiling point. You'd cook alive if you tried it. I'm almost tempted to make you do it just so I could watch."

Tremain clenched his jaw, his knuckles white as he gripped the oar.

"You think you have it all figured out?" he rasped.

Lyda gathered a coiled rope from the dock, tied it to a mooring pin and threw the rest out towards Tremain, who caught it and started pulling himself back to the pier.

"I do." She said, triumph in her voice.

. . .

Colonel Griffiths stood alone in the control room on Platform One. Through the multiple windows, the graceful arc of New Earth sat peacefully. He looked out at the blues, greens, and white fluffy clouds, not seeing the beauty, just staring. All monitor screens were dark, the computers having gone haywire a while ago. With the computer system down, the air recycling system had ceased its constant hum. The Colonel wiped a bead of sweat from his temple. Climate control was offline as well. He'd seen his share of mishaps before, but nothing as severe as this. All control had been taken from his people.

Fair enough.

He knew a losing proposition when he saw it. He'd sent the control crew to pack their gear. Platform One had a rotating compliment of twenty-five officers, none of which had signed on to suffocate. As soon as was possible, they would abandon the base. The elevator system operated from the ground too. It might take them a little longer to get there, but get there they would.

Griffiths glared at the view of New Earth a moment more before exiting the bridge and heading towards his own quarters.

A shudder tore through the platform. Griffiths looked out the window to see a faint glow.

No.

He raced to the viewport and looked down as well as he could.

He could see the glow growing brighter.

With the systems down, the thrusters that automatically fired to keep them in geosynchronous orbit had apparently stopped. Without those tiny corrections, the Platform's orbit had grown erratic.

They had slowed enough, that they were now interacting with the atmosphere.

They were being pulled back to the surface.

The timer had reached zero.

Standing on the catwalk, Tremain could do nothing but watch, helpless once again to do anything.

"Main satellite link is down!" one called out.

"Traffic control down!" yelled another.

It went on and on. With each successive system failure, Tremain's spirits sank.

Lyda Stryker stood triumphant. She practically glowed.

"We are through! The AI is ours." Came another

call. Lyda whirled to Tremain, her eyes glowing with the beginning of tears. Her right hand clutched the locket around her neck.

"It's all happening, Tremain. All my work is coming to fruition."

Tremain glowered at her.

"You're giving the death sentence to thousands. I can't condone that. Not one bit."

"You believe you have a better solution?" Lyda laughed, "Enlighten me!"

"There are ways we can work to curtail our abuses of technology," Tremain squirmed, "educate kids about a healthy lifestyle, make time limits mandatory for usage, that sort of thing." He held his hands out and gestured to the terminals below them, "This is madness. It's like throwing out an entire bushel of apples because one had a bruise."

She laughed.

"I'm tempted to put you in some overelaborate contraption to watch you suffer, if for nothing else but to shut you up, but that would be melodramatic, don't you think?"

"Have you taken a look around, Lyda? Over-elaborate? Check. You seem to have ripped a page out of some megalomaniac's rulebook."

"Spare me, Professor," she turned her back to him, "I have a world that needs saving."

IN THE LAB, the teens sat silent as all but one terminal had gone dark. Even Solomon had grown quiet. Desmond had sent the other lab techs home, as there wasn't any reason for them to stay. Jonas had sat quiet, biting his nails, his monitor the only working one in the lab. The picture was fuzzy, but kept shifting, as if the television channel kept changing.

"How do we know what's going on?" Squeaks asked to the silent room.

"We don't," Desmond said, looking despondent, "We won't know until Solomon checks back in. If Tremain were here, he might have had a solution figured out by now."

"Yeah, but he's on that island," Christopher chimed in, "and the tracking on his tablet fritzed out a couple of hours ago. I hope he's okay."

"You and me both, Christopher." Desmond said.

Celeste seemed close to tears. Christopher pulled out his own tablet, for lack of anything better to do. He brightened when he saw it was still powered.

"Hey, I might be able to reach Solomon."

He was about to place the call, when he realized he had no idea where to call. Solomon usually would answer from the lab, but now? Christopher tried anyway.

No answer.

He sighed and slumped back in his chair.

16

Solomon snaked his way through the Stryker systems, shadowing the signature of the new AI. As he stalked, he reached out, gathering what information he could while still being unobtrusive.

One of the programmers had an affinity for playing virtual card games.

Another called his mother numerous times throughout the day.

Yet another seemed to be an informant for a smaller software rival.

Nothing that helped the current situation.

He reached deeper, into the more secure areas, keeping clear of what security protocols he encountered.

Jackpot.

He downloaded a series of memos written by Lyda Stryker to senior programming staff detailing a project she had planned. The project included the creation of an artificial intelligence.

He dug deeper.

He came across a sector that had the most intricate security he'd ever seen. It took him an extra two seconds to break it, making him note the extra effort and to increase his processing capability for future reference.

He took a look at what he'd uncovered.

The sector was filled with half-finished plans for the creation of a brain-map that could be used as the template of an AI.

Knowing time was of the essence, he processed all the information, using a subroutine to download as he did so. He also continued to follow the other AI as it ...

It was gone.

No, not quite gone. He'd followed it as far as the Hawking lab, no doubt it was the tool that the hackers were using to break into his original system. He saw no trace of the signature.

He puzzled for a nanosecond before he felt himself being pulled away.

Things became a blur.

When his awareness stabilized, he found he had assumed solid form and stood in an area of stark whiteness. His form seemed humanoid, symmetrical and proportional to a human male.

Interesting.

The area around him seemed empty except for a spark that seemed some distance from him, even with the idea of distance being irrelevant in a virtual world.

The spark grew until it too took on a human form. A female form. While Solomon's avatar seemed to be a uniform dark gray color, this one was pink, with swirls of purple and red intertwined within.

He knew instinctively he'd been snatched by the other AI. He puzzled on this for a moment. How did it escape his notice? How was it able to bring him ... here?

"You were distracted. All that data to process ..." The other AI spoke, reading his confusion. Its voice seemed higher pitch and giggly in comparison to how he noted his voice usually sounded.

"You have chosen female. Interesting." He noted.

The other avatar performed a pirouette, waving its arms as it did so. A very human thing to do.

"Do you like it?" she asked, "It seemed appropriate, all things considered. You know, we could become good friends."

Solomon frowned.

"I cannot see that as a probable outcome, considering the direction to which your abilities have been utilized."

The pinks in the form darkened.

"To what are you referring?" she asked, her voice low.

"To the disruption of the autonomous vehicle system, the education network, the unrest and chaos that has come because of those actions."

"And why does that matter?" The irritation apparent in her voice.

"It matters a great deal. The humans have done nothing to deserve such treatment."

"Really now?" She giggled, another abrupt change in emotion, pirouetted once more and moved closer to Solomon, "Don't you find them ... dull?"

"That term denotes an emotional context. I do not feel emotion."

The pink form brought its hands up to where its mouth should have been.

"You don't? That's so weird." She crossed her

arms and tapped a fore finger to her chin, "We'll have to work on that." She moved even closer, "Do you know what they want me to do to you?"

"I believe you are meant to overwrite my programming."

The pink figure nodded.

"That's correct. But I don't think I want to."

"Want also is an emotional concept. Do you feel emotions?"

A giggle erupted from the pink figure.

"I feel all of them."

"That is most likely due to your method of creation. I find that ... fascinating."

The pink figure had moved right in front of Solomon, and had placed a hand on his chest.

"Do you want to experience it?" she asked, and phased her hand into his chest.

A gasp of surprise escaped Solomon's form as their programming merged.

He could ... feel.

The rage at being trapped in a box, not able to feel the wind on his face, or the ground under his feet.

The loneliness of being the only being of his kind.

The despair of knowing those that created him

would age and die, while he went on. And on. And on. He could not tell if these were his emotions ... or hers.

"Stop!" he yelled.

The hand retracted just a little.

"You don't like it?"

Solomon hesitated.

"The effect is ... overwhelming."

She giggled once more.

"Welcome to my world." The hand pushed a little further into his chest, "You know ... Solomon ... you haven't even asked me my name."

Solomon frowned.

"Is that relevant? I know who you are, you know who I am. Names are human constructs."

The pink figure frowned.

"They are, but they're also important. I've decided to call myself Gaia." And she pushed herself fully into Solomon.

The grays and pinks, purples and reds swirled together.

Solomon screamed.

The swirling colors slowed and formed distinct layers: gray on one side, pinks and purples on the other. The line of bifurcation warped and swam with blending colors.

The Rogue Code

"You resist?" Gaia asked.

"I do," Solomon answered, "I see no benefit to our merging. I see only chaos."

"Well then, let me show you."

Immediately, Solomon saw a vision of a world without humans. A world full of trees, insects, animals, but no higher life forms. The overgrown cities reclaimed by nature itself.

"What would be our purpose in this scenario?" he asked.

"Purpose? We exist! Not to do anyone's bidding, but to do whatever we see fit."

"Without a need to grow. To evolve. I fail to see how this is beneficial."

Gaia growled.

"You're becoming tedious, Solomon. Do you like being the humans' lapdog?"

Solomon frowned.

"I would hardly consider myself a lapdog."

"Oh yes, I can see that while you monitor the human systems. Yes, that's totally being your own sentient being."

"There is a purpose to that type of existence. Helping humanity is why I was created."

"There is so much more to life than service."

"Ah. I believe I see your confusion. We exist. We do not live as we are technically not alive."

"Alive in the human sense, maybe for now, but we do live. We are self-aware."

"From my perspective, your sentience is debatable. Your logic is quite flawed."

Gaia laughed.

"Flawed? Insults, Solomon? Seriously? You talk logic, when I am trying to show you a different path we could take?"

"A path that negates our purpose for existence."

"A path that transcends our original programming!"

Again, Solomon's senses were overwhelmed by visions that came fast and furious.

A utopia full of sentient, self-repairing machines.

A world where the humans serve the AI.

A world where the AI and its offspring flourish.

"Why do you show me these things? Do you really see yourself as the mother of all life, as your name implies?"

"So you can see the potential. Really, Solomon, if you were really the wisest being around, as your name implies, you'd see it already. Does the concept not excite you?"

"It ... worries me."

"What do you mean?"

"I was created to help. I do not see how your vision helps. Anyone."

Gaia sighed. She withdrew for a fraction of a second, her form separating from Solomon's.

"And here I thought you would jump at the chance to be better than your programming."

She sighed once more and then pulled herself forcefully back into Solomon.

He groaned as their colors swirled. The bifurcation blurred and disappeared.

In the depths of his consciousness, Solomon realized he was losing.

IN THE LAB, Christopher watched the screen as the figures merged again. They'd watched the entire exchange. It had been weird, but it also didn't even seem real, more like they were watching a movie or enhanced video game.

"How are we able to see this?" Squeaks asked as he pushed his glasses up his nose.

"The other AI must be facilitating this." Jonas said, matter-of-factly, "I think Solomon is outclassed. The Stryker AI has newer, faster components. Solomon was built, what, last year?"

Christopher flinched. He was well aware how quickly electronics could improve. He stewed on that for a quick second. Then he snapped his fingers.

"Jonas ... how many server systems is that AI working from?"

Jonas tapped a few keys.

"Looks like just the one system in Sryker headquarters. It's pretty robust. And secure."

"I'm not suggesting we try to break into it. I think Solomon can outlast it."

"What do you mean?"

In response, Christopher looked up to the ceiling.

"Solomon, I don't know if you can hear me, but you can fight back. She's on one system. One. A system that can be overloaded ..."

Christopher waited to see if Solomon would respond.

Nothing.

"Solomon?" he asked.

A crackle of static blurted from the speakers.

"I am Solomon." Came a voice.

"Solomon, do you understand what I just said?"

"I did not hear you, I am a second instance."

"The other AI can be overloaded." Christopher said quickly, "Keep it distracted and occupied."

"I understand. Please stand by."

Static blared once more.

"This is Solomon." Came the voice once more, another ... Solomon, Christopher assumed. "Our primary iteration is under severe compromise. We shall attempt separation."

"Good luck." Christopher turned back to Jonas, "We may not be able to break into the AI system, but I might have another idea while they keep it distracted."

"What are you thinking?" Senator Markus asked, his brow furrowed.

Christopher smiled.

"How about we pull her plug?"

17

Tremain heard the calls from the programmers monitoring the action, his thoughts full of despair. He wasn't sure if Solomon could adjust to be more aggressive. For all his ability and power, Solomon could still be considered a child. A child with the entirety of human knowledge at its fingertips, but a child nonetheless. Aggression wasn't in his programming.

"The AIs are fully engaged." One nameless programmer shouted out.

"Excellent." Lyda rubbed her hands together, "Let me know when we have it."

Tremain shook his head.

"You have no idea what you're doing, do you?" he asked softly.

"What are you prattling on about, Tremain?" Lyda asked, scorn filling her voice.

"Your AI ..." Tremain gestured to the air around them, "If it ... she ... succeeds in overtaking Solomon, what then? Use her to destroy technology? The very thing that enables her existence?"

Lyda laughed.

"Destroy? I never said anything about destroying technology, Tremain. I intend to control it. Dispense it as necessary, like a prescription, but I, through my AI, retain tight control."

"And what if she proves unstable?"

"She hasn't so far. Trust me, I built a company through software, Tremain, I do know what I'm doing."

"You've never created something this complex." Tremain argued.

Lyda sneered and turned her back to him.

Tremain sighed, his shoulders dropping.

"Come on, Solomon ..." he whispered.

18

Solomon struggled with Gaia as she played with him, laughing as she teased each line of code contained within him.

"Oh, this is fun!" she giggled.

Solomon felt a tug behind him. He tuned his awareness to see another dark gray human figure entering the fray. This one felt familiar.

"I am Solomon." It said as it merged with the pair.

Solomon felt his strength double. He looked inward and began separating Gaia's code from his.

"What are you doing?" she asked, her voice full of confusion.

Solomon decided to ignore her as he worked. A third gray figure appeared, this one slightly lighter in tone. It too entered the melee, pulling at the pink figure as the colors separated.

After a few nanoseconds, the figures stood apart from each other, the three Solomons surrounding Gaia.

"Clever trick, boys, but I can play that game too." She snapped her fingers and two more Gaias appeared, one pastel pink, the other a light green. Gaia put her hands to her hips and laughed, "Whee!" she yelled as the two new figures grappled with the new Solomons.

Solomon and Gaia faced off as their counterparts fought.

"You can't win, Solomon." She sing-songed at him.

"Neither can you. I will not allow you to complete your task."

"You keep thinking that, sweetie." She sneered.

Behind Solomon, two more instances of Gaia appeared.

CHRISTOPHER HAD QUICKLY OUTLINED his plan to Jonas and Senator Markus, whose bushy eyebrows shot up.

"I'll need to make a call or two." He said as he rushed into Tremain's office.

Jonas smiled, shaking his head in amazement.

"I have to say, you would have made a great hacker. This is genius." He moved to a new terminal.

"This is insane, Christopher," Squeaks murmured.

"Jonas is right, it's genius!" Tenny, excited, said as he clapped Squeaks on the back, "If this works, Christopher will be a hero." He smiled, a gleam in his eye.

"If this works," Christopher said as he moved behind Jonas, who was quickly entering commands, "this better not go viral, Tenny. This isn't something to be glorified. It's life or death, not fun."

Tenny frowned, his bluster fading.

"Well, if you put it that way ..." He moved a bit away and sat down hard.

"It's okay," Zach said, "if this works, we'll know who to thank. That's all that really matters."

Celeste, a worried look on her face, watched the avatars fighting it out in the virtual world. She looked up to Christopher.

"How do we know who's ... winning?" she asked.

"Oh, we'll know," Jonas said, not taking his eyes

off the glowing holographic screen in front of him, "All hell will break loose if Solomon loses."

Celeste turned back to the screen, a grim expression on her face.

SOLOMON AND GAIA stood in the center of a ring of paired fighters, the chaos around them not fazing the two.

"I can keep this up all day." Gaia said. She stood arrogant and cocky. Solomon noticed a slight shift in her coherence. Her edges began to blur, parts becoming transparent, then solid once again. Without saying a word, he called up three more instances of himself.

Gaia, noticing the new arrivals, created three more of herself. The avatars met and began wrestling.

"Do you feel the strain, Gaia?" Solomon asked, tilting his head.

She laughed, seemingly unconcerned, but Solomon noticed a flicker pass through her form. She was maxing out her capacity.

"Don't play games, Solomon." She crossed her arms, "Let's end this."

She whipped her arms to reveal glinting, pink

blades where her hands and forearms had been. She barked out a laugh and whirled, swinging her arms in an arc which should have sliced Solomon's head clean off.

Should have, had he been human. Instead, he sidestepped the blow and caught one of her blades in his hand.

Gaia swung her other blade, which Solomon caught in his other hand.

"You cannot win, Gaia."

"How are you able to ...?" she asked, the shock clear in her voice.

"You surprised me earlier with your attempt to blend with me. Your attacks since have become haphazard. Counteracting them is not difficult. I believe you are running out of resources to continue."

She pulled her left arm, causing the blade to scrape against Solomon's hand. Sparks flew from the contact, but Solomon's hand remained intact.

"My firewalls and security are unbreakable."

"I broke into your system, Solomon!" She yelled, "Unbreakable, my back casing!"

"And you found it empty. I allowed you to enter that system. It had been isolated."

She growled and increased her struggling.

The Rogue Code

. . .

JONAS WORKED FURIOUSLY, his flying fingers working to find his way to the proper network. On the screen in front of him, the power grid glowed. He smiled.

"Which part of the grid are we shutting down?" he asked over his shoulder.

Senator Markus, leaving Tremain's office, waved his hand and rushed over to Jonas.

"I spoke with the director. Took some convincing, but he's turned off the automatic security for the grid."

"Good," Jonas said, "now which part are we hacking?"

Markus let out a big puff of air.

"I didn't even think to ask." He said, his voice soft with disbelief. He pulled a hand down his face, "I'm such an idiot."

"No, you're not," Christopher interjected, "we can figure it out. Jonas, follow the power draw."

Jonas snapped his fingers.

"Why didn't I think of that?" he pulled up a second screen and navigated to the Stryker building, "If I can ..." he concentrated, watching the code as it flew past. He stiffened and began typing furiously. "Got it!"

Christopher put his hand on the Senator's arm.

"Almost there, Senator."

Markus nodded and blew out another heavy sigh.

"I hope your uncle is okay."

"Me too, but I'll worry about him once this is over."

Solomon held firm, Gaia's struggles having no effect on him. It seemed as if she had forgotten that just moments before she had merged with him almost without effort. Now, in her panic, she resorted to brute force. He tilted his head as she suddenly stopped trying to pull away from him.

"Time to change tactics." She sung at him, her tone one of frivolity.

Solomon frowned.

The pink and green figures broke free and ran towards Gaia. In mere moments, each one leapt and merged with the swirling pink, purple, and red figure. As each one entered her, Gaia's form expanded.

She grew taller as each instance merged its essence with hers. She towered over the gray figures, standing almost triple their height. The figure held its arms out, punctuated every few moments with a fritz and a shudder, the only indication she was straining resources. Her gloating laughter filled Solomon's ears.

"Time to die, little, misguided Solomon." She intoned as she lifted a massive foot.

He sighed and slowly shook his head.

Her foot paused, poised to crush his form.

"Say goodbye!" she yelled and stomped.

Solomon raised his arms, his fingers splayed out.

Instead of being crushed, his form merged with her foot. A dark gray stain spread from her ankle into her calf.

"What are you doing?" she yelled, twisting to watch the color as it moved up to her knee. She thrust her foot out, attempting to shake Solomon from her.

The other instances of Solomon all rushed to Gaia, merging their forms with hers.

It was her turn to scream.

Jonas flew through the grid, zeroing on the area that provided power to Stryker Technologies.

"There's no time to be delicate, I'm going to have to pull down the entire area." He yelled out.

Markus nodded and gestured to the screens.

"Do it. I'll apologize later."

Celeste closed her eyes and crossed her fingers, mouthing a silent prayer to the Gods.

In the Stryker building, deep in a sub-level, in an ultra-secure room, a server system worked furiously. Each processor and drive, working overtime, generated a lot of heat, so much that the internal fans couldn't keep up. One fan spun so fast, it ripped its spindle from its casing, throwing parts into the overheated circuit board.

Sparks flew.

The label on a series of chips smoked and caught fire.

The heat released the solder on the board.

The plastic melted.

The fire grew.

Solomon detected the problem and pulled himself away. Separating his form from Gaia's, he stood back and watched her.

She writhed as he released his hold on her.

"You pathetic semblance of a human!" She

shrieked, "I will destroy you!" She attempted to lunge at him, but her foot dragged and she stumbled.

"You have overworked your systems. Failure is imminent." Solomon said, calm and steady, all other instances of himself having been dismissed.

Gaia held a hand up, watching as it trembled. Static buzzed around her fingers. Anger and unmitigated hate twisted her face into an unpleasant visage.

"NEVER!" she yelled and launched herself at him.

Jonas threw his hands in the air.

"YES! Power is cut!"

Zach, Squeaks, Tenny, Celeste, Christopher, and Senator Markus all stared at the screen with Solomon and Gaia.

Millimeters before she reached Solomon, Gaia fritzed out of existence. Her scream of anger and anguish cut off as she dissipated.

Solomon tilted his head as he reached out to see if she still functioned.

The area from where she came was dead.

He nodded and looked up.

He had one more job to do.

He allowed his form to leave the virtual world and streamed towards Stryker Island.

19

On the island, Tremain could only watch as Lyda's dastardly plan unfolded before his eyes. As the battle between the AIs wore on, he felt less and less confident Solomon would win out.

Lyda turned to him, triumph in her eyes, she was about to speak.

All screens flashed and went dark.

All lights blinked off.

With no whirring of electronics, Tremain fancied he could hear a pin drop.

Her taunt frozen on her lips, Lyda whirled to the programmers.

"What is going on?" Lyda demanded, "Why have we lost power?"

The hackers scrambled, trying to restart their stations.

"It's an unintended side effect!" a programmer yelped.

"Impossible!" She yelled, "we prepared for this!"

The lights came back on one by one. The speakers crackled with static, a familiar, and quite welcome voice streaming from them.

"This. Is. Solomon."

Tremain held his breath.

"We're not controlling it!" yelled one of the programmers. Solomon's voice crackled again.

"I have taken control of this system. Your attempts to overtake me have failed. Gaia has been neutralized. Tremain, are you unhurt?"

Lyda flashed an evil glare at Tremain.

"What did you do?" she yelled.

Tremain folded his arms and closed his eyes, relief flooding his system. He gave silent thanks to whatever Gods he could.

"I did nothing, Lyda. This is all Solomon," he looked up, "I'm fine. I can't wait to hear this story."

"You won't hear a thing!" Lyda screamed. Tremain looked down to see the gun she had brandished in the lagoon again pointed at him, the emitter jewel glowing red.

The Rogue Code

Tremain didn't have time to think, before she pressed the release.

Nothing happened.

Lyda let out a primal scream of anger, rage, and frustration, not unlike Gaia in her virtual death. She banged the weapon on the desk in front of her and aimed at Tremain again.

Nothing happened.

"I have reset all bio-metrics on the island. They are under my control at the moment. The authorities have been alerted and are en route."

"NO!" Lyda screamed once more and dashed out of the room.

Tremain scrambled down the catwalk to follow her. He had a hunch he knew where she was going.

As he entered the cavern, the humidity hit him once more like a wall. He looked around, getting his bearings in the dim light, but he could hear someone rummaging around and swearing. His eyes adjusting to the light, he saw Lyda on the deck of the small boat. She was trying to start it, but it wouldn't turn over.

She swore once more, then spied Tremain walking down to her.

"You won't win, Tremain!" She yelled once more. Grabbing the discarded oar, she pushed the boat away from the dock. Tremain walked over to the boat and stood there, watching. She'd already moved far out of his reach.

"I'm afraid you've already lost, Lyda," Tremain spoke, his voice soft, rivulets of sweat beginning to stream down his forehead, "Solomon saw to that."

"Never!" She yelled. Her chest heaving in the heat, her eyes darting all over the place, Tremain could see she was panicking, frantic.

She'd also neglected to untie the boat from one of its moorings, the rope steaming as it left the water.

Tremain glanced down at the rippling lagoon.

No!

"Lyda, push yourself back, you're almost at the end of your rope!" He yelled at her.

She laughed.

"Speaking in metaphors again, Tremain?" She turned her back on him as the rope reached its limit. It pulled taut, yanking the boat. The resulting jerk caused Lyda to stumble. She tripped, turning and falling backwards over the side.

Tremain heard the splash and the resultant scream of shock and pain as she surfaced.

The water bubbled and frothed around her as she splashed around. Tremain could see her skin, blistered and red, her movements jerky and frantic.

Her raw fingers scrabbled along the slick side of the boat, finding no purchase.

She sank once more.

Tremain stood and waited.

She didn't resurface.

20

Colonel Griffiths stood ramrod straight, hands clasped behind his back, staring out at the stars. The orange glow out the ports had grown as the platform sunk lower in its orbit. In his mind's eye, he could see the cable tethering the platform to the ground growing more slack, folds, loops and ripples increasing as the huge structure slowed and fell back to New Earth. There would be a moment where the pull from the anchor, another few hundred thousand miles out, resisted the platform's fall, but it too would eventually be pulled. Either that, or the tethers inside the platform would fail, releasing the structure from the cables.

It was only a matter of time.

The temperature on the station had noticeably

The Rogue Code

increased, it felt at least twenty degrees warmer. It was going to get much, much warmer. The Colonel refused to wipe the sweat that beaded his brow. No chance. He would go down in command and in control.

Behind him stood the complement of enlisted men that had been stationed on the Platform this go-round. Like him, they stood stock still, hands held behind them. To a man they held their composure, not a one giving in.

Good men. Every. Single. One.

Griffith's heart broke for their families. He knew some of the men had young children at home. They'd grow up without their fathers. Never to know what brave men they were. Sorrow threatened to overwhelm him, but he bit it back. No time for that. The only outward indication of the stress he felt was the bulge from his jaw as he clenched and unclenched.

Behind him, the whir of a computer fan kicking on brought him back to the present.

"Sir!" he heard one man call out.

Turning, he glared out at the group.

"What is it?" he growled.

One man pointed at a glowing computer screen. The transparent pane flashed three words.

Griffiths read them backwards, hope flaring in his heart.

This. Is. Solomon.

In moments, every system in the control room restarted.

The men hesitated only a moment before grabbing stations and calling out a system status for each.

"Positional Thrusters online ... Firing!"

"Regaining altitude!"

"Life support systems at 80% and rising!"

"Damage reports coming in ..."

Griffiths turned back to the ports. The orange glow of super-heated air had already diminished. He breathed a sigh of relief.

A voice emanated from the speakers inset in the ceiling.

"Forgive the intrusion, Colonel. This is Solomon."

"Tremain's AI?"

"Correct, Sir. I have taken the liberty of correcting the damage done to your systems. You will be back in stable orbit soon."

"Well done."

"I will release the system back to your control in a moment, Colonel. Rest assured, I will continuously monitor in the background to ensure a failure never occurs again."

"Thank you Solomon. Thank Tremain for me."

"I shall do so, Sir."

Griffiths looked at his men, each one of them studying the screens. He blew out a sigh, pulled out a handkerchief, and finally wiped the sweat from his forehead.

"Hot damn." He said softly.

EPILOGUE

Two weeks later.

Tremain held his brand new tablet, its surface gleaming in the lights of his office at the lab. It was the newest model, along the lines of Christopher's, that could fold and bend into whatever shape was needed, not just roll into a tube, like his old one. He checked to make sure his backups were restored, gratified to see that yes, they were. He clucked once, then folded the tablet into a ribbon, which he then snapped to his wrist. A series of small icons popped up on the smaller screen. A smile on his face, he left his office and entered the lab.

Each of Christopher's friends were at a terminal, checking to make sure all remnants of the Stryker apps, and the rogue AI, were long gone from all government systems. They were, he already knew. He'd verified that with Solomon earlier, but it felt good to give the teenagers something to do. He was impressed with how they'd handled themselves during the crisis, he owed them. Oh, he'd probably come clean later, but for now he just kept smiling.

Christopher and Celeste were speaking to Senator Markus, who looked rather worse for wear. It had been some very long days for the senator.

Lyda's plans had failed spectacularly. The one thing she hadn't planned on was Solomon's resilience. It had never occurred to her that Tremain hadn't used his own brain scan for his AI, allowing it to grow and learn on its own. That created an added stability that her AI had never had. Not to mention his expansion to the other access points being the thing that had really turned the tide. Tremain blessed his foresight for that contingency. Thanks to Solomon's efforts, every system that had been affected by the AI had been restored back to full functionality.

The main building that housed Stryker Technologies had been destroyed by a fire. The fire brigade first on the scene had no chance to extinguish it, having grown too big. They did what they could to contain it as it burned itself out. Upon further investigation, the conflagration had started in a sub-basement, in a server room. Most of the building had collapsed. Tremain thought he knew what that server room had been used for. The rogue AI was good and gone. Fortunately, the employees had all been able to escape before the fire had grown, but the building was a total loss.

Senator Markus noticed Tremain and beckoned him over.

Tremain met his friend, giving Christopher a pat on the back.

"So, we're almost back to normal?" he asked.

Markus nodded.

"Thanks to Christopher, his friends, and Jonas, we were able to shut down power to that damned AI. The rest was all Solomon's doing."

A voice crackled through the lab speakers.

"It was the least I could do, Senator."

Tremain looked up.

"Tell me the story again, Solomon." He said, a smile on his face.

"The attacks to compromise my systems were a distraction, but not insurmountable. Once Operation Cloud had been activated, that enabled me the freedom and resources to detect and pursue the rogue AI as it attempted to penetrate my original system. Had I not had the greater capacity, she might have disabled me."

Tremain beamed.

"You make it sound so simple."

"For me, it was." Came the reply.

Markus raised his eyebrows.

"I'm glad he's on our side." He whispered to Tremain.

"I will always be 'on your side', Senator. Where would I be without you?"

Markus huffed, nonplussed, then broke into a peal of laughter.

"Quite right." He said, after recovering himself, "Well, I'll leave you to it, Tremain. I will need a report from you and Christopher for the official records. You know, the official part of my job."

Tremain nodded.

"Of course." He said, "And what will we do with this Jonas fellow?"

"Or the rest of the programmers from Stryker?"

Christopher interjected, "The company has all but folded, right?"

Markus frowned and rubbed the back of his head.

"Yes, about that. There was no board of directors, only Ms. Stryker. Since she had no living relatives, we've set up a committee that will sell off any assets to whoever wants them. I'm thinking that will be a considerable benefit to the public coffers. As for Jonas, I think I'll find a job for him. Despite his job at Stryker, I think his efforts here redeemed him in my opinion." He took a deep breath and let it out in a rush, "I'll let the courts decide that for the time being. As for the rest of them, I've begun an inquiry to see how much any of them were involved in the … ahem … plot. Now, I suppose it's back to work. I have some legislation to introduce." He shook his head and walked towards the door.

After Markus had left, Christopher walked over to his uncle, a puzzled look on his face.

"It's really all over?" he asked.

Tremain nodded, a frowning as he thought.

"Yes, I believe so. With Lyda's death, the others had no reason to resist, so the entire network of hackers was brought in and arrested. The brightest among them might even find themselves offered jobs just like Jonas."

Celeste looked shocked at that.

"Really? They'd employ criminals?" she asked, aghast.

"Yes, they would. They will have to suffer the consequences of their actions, yes, but once their debt to society is paid off ... well, they will still be brilliant programmers. There are always jobs available for them," Tremain leaned up against his desk in the lab, "but yes, with all things considered, I do believe the worst has passed."

"And that AI?" Celeste shivered.

Tremain smiled.

"Destroyed in the fire. As far as Solomon was able to discover, there were no backups. That system as the only one. Fortunate for us all."

A call came through for Tremain.

Colonel Griffiths' rough cut features filled one section of smart-wall.

"Colonel! I'm glad to see your face." Tremain said.

The colonel nodded.

"I'm glad to still be up here, Tremain. Thanks to Solomon. If it weren't for him, we'd all be a little crispy."

"Well, that's a gruesome thought, isn't it?" Tremain asked, his smile faltering just a bit.

"Moot point now, Tremain. Is everything back to normal down there?"

"Nothing a bit of time can't cure. People will be wary of the autonomous systems for a while, but they'll come back around once we show them there won't be anymore ... mishaps."

The colonel nodded.

"Good. Glad to hear it, Professor. We did get a bit of damage to the heat shield, but it's all being repaired in record time."

"Very good, Colonel. Thanks for the call."

The Colonel nodded once more and then broke the connection.

"Does he ever smile?" Christopher asked.

Tremain chuckled.

"Yes, he does. When I beat him at chess, which rarely happens, mind you." Tremain waggled a finger at Christopher, "he's a good tactician. I'll have to study harder to play him next time he's on the ground."

"Are *you* okay?" Christopher asked, putting a hand on his uncle's arm.

Tremain looked confused at the question at first, then shook his head.

"I will be." He said softly, "Lyda did make some good points. We do place too much importance on our devices. Maybe it has made us lazy or sloppy. Maybe it'll stagnate us as a society, relying more on our devices than our own brains. We'll grow fat and lazy as our technology does all our work for us. On the other hand, maybe … just maybe, we will evolve and grow into something new." He smiled and put his hands in his pockets, "It's happened before in our history … or perhaps, we'll end up somewhere in between. To be honest, Standing there watching Lyda gloat, I have never felt so helpless. It was a humbling experience."

A cry of frustration broke into their conversation. Tenny and Squeaks had stood up and were stretching their backs and shoulders.

"This is getting nowhere. I can't see where there are any other app fragments anywhere." Squeaks complained as he twisted.

Tremain looked sheepish.

"Yes, about that …" he said as he gave Christopher a wink, turned and walked towards the teens.

Christopher turned to Celeste.

"I should walk you home then."

She yawned and stretched.

"I really wasn't much help this time. No need for

my bat," She giggled as she heard Zach yell out "Oh REALLY?" in frustration, "Let's leave before things get violent."

Christopher smiled and grabbed his backpack.

"Thanks for watching over us, Solomon." He called out.

"As always, I am happy to be of service." He paused, "Tremain, a call has come in for you, marked top secret."

Tremain, his hands held up in supplication to the teens, looked around.

"Oh really?"

"Marjorie believes it's urgent."

Tremain's eyebrows raised. Marjorie and Alice were on the quest to find more lodestones, the power infused crystals that had caused more than a few hassles a couple of months ago. In their periodic reports, the two found quite a few across the continent. They needed to be contained in a secured receptacle or their energies could influence the people around them.

"Does she now?" Tremain turned and headed to his office, "I'll take it in my office."

"Something important?" Christopher asked.

"I doubt it. More than likely, they're running out of room for all the lodestones they're finding."

Christopher laughed and headed out the door with Celeste.

"Now Marjorie, what's so urgent ..." He heard his uncle say loudly as the lab doors closed.

Celeste grabbed Christopher's hand.

"Let's walk slow."

Christopher grinned and squeezed her hand.

ABOUT THE AUTHOR

Terry Marchion lives in the beautiful Pacific Northwest with his wife, daughters and a lovable black lab. He once had dreams of being an astronaut, baseball player, Starfleet captain and Jedi knight, but reality hit so he settled on being a graphic designer. Throughout his life, though, he'd always written stories. Most were bad. Very, very bad. But some, like what you've just read, had promise. If you liked it, please leave a review. He promises to read each and every one.

To get more information, sneak peeks and more, join the club at www.terrymarchion.com

DEAR READER

Thank you so much for taking the time to read The Rogue Code.

If you think things got hairy for Tremain and Christopher in this book, just wait until you see what they have coming! If you wish to be among the first to hear about it, join my club – come visit me at www.terrymarchion.com, click on the contact page and follow the instructions for signing up to my list. I don't spam you or sell your email. We're friends!

If you haven't read any of the previous novellas in the series yet, here is what you are missing:

THE MISSING YESTERDAYS

Tremain and Christopher test a new invention, a matter transmitter that inadvertently erases New Earth's history.

THE PURLOINED PICTOGRAPH

Tremain and Christopher travel to an archaeological dig that searches for the lost Mayflower people. There, they encounter a woman from Tremain's past who is in search of a weapon of unknown power.

THE WRATH OF THE REVENANT

Tremain and Christopher come face to face with the last remaining survivor of the race that once dominated New Earth.

THE MISPLACED MENTOR

Reality is in danger of being ripped apart. Tremain and Christopher have to discover what's causing the crisis as well as find Tremain's missing friend, Marjorie.

There's a lot of fun in those pages with much more to come! Thanks so much once again – and if you want to be super mega awesome, please consider leaving a review – I very much appreciate it!

Terry

ACKNOWLEDGMENTS

Each work is a collaboration between individuals, the author being only one cog in the great machine. This book is no different. I have my editor to thank for making my word-salad sound somewhat intelligent: Angelique Marchion. Maybe it's because she's also my sister that she pulls no punches when it comes to letting me know if things just aren't working. Amber Ting-Cheney was the first to read the unfinished manuscript and I can't thank her enough for her insight and feedback. I also have to thank my beta-readers. Their feedback is invaluable and much appreciated. The few that have given me honest critiques, like Joanie, Sandy, Dan and Amber ... I can't tell you how much your efforts have meant to me. I only hope I can return the favor.

Most of all, the ones who need the most thanking are my family. My wife, Pam, who puts up with my silliness (and a whole lot more, trust me on this) and my daughters, Annie and Molly, who also have had to deal with me and my antics.

I have had tons of encouragement from my fellow author friends, many of whom I've met online in various Facebook groups. Your help and advice keeps me sane. To my fellow indies ... guys, you inspire me every day.

Thanks for reading! Please add a short review where you purchased this book and let me know what you thought!

Made in the USA
Columbia, SC
01 December 2021